the Secret of the Floating Phantom

The Secret of the Floating Phantom

Norma Lehr

 Lerner Publications Company • Minneapolis

Library of Congress Cataloging-in-Publication Data

Lehr, Norma.
    The secret of the floating phantom / Norma Lehr.
        p.   cm.
    Summary: While staying with her grandmother in Monterey,
California, eleven-year-old Kathy has some strange experiences as
she is led by a foglike phantom to a treasure hidden from pirates over
150 years ago.
    ISBN 0-8225-0736-6
    [1. Mystery and detective stories. 2. Ghosts—Fiction.
3. Monterey (Calif.)—Fiction. 4. Grandmothers—Fiction.]
    I. Title.
PZ7.L53273Se   1994
[Fic]—dc20   94-3004
                                                                CIP
                                                                 AC

Manufactured in the United States of America

1 2 3 4 5 6 I/JR 99 98 97 96 95 94

For David and Eileen,
in loving memory

CHAPTER
1

"How am I supposed to help Gram?" Kathy asked her dad. "Gram's a dance teacher." Kathy poked around in her potato salad, removed a sliver of onion with a prong of her fork, and examined it closely. "I can't tap dance, you know."

Kathy's father shook his head and smiled. "That's not why Grandma Bev wants you to visit. Someone else will teach her classes. She wants to spend some time with you while she's laid up with that twisted knee. You can help with the shopping and errands, though, can't you?"

"Sure. I guess. But you didn't bring my bike, and if Gram can't drive...." She placed the fork next to her dish, then leaned across the booth and peered at her dad's plate. "Can I have one of your fries?"

"You can have them all," he said, motioning for a waitress. "I'll ask for a doggy bag. You can eat them while we drive."

On the way to the car, Kathy thought about home. It seemed like forever since she'd been in her own neighborhood. She'd just spent a month at Aunt Sharon's. Her dad picked her up there and now she was on her way to Gram's. Kathy knew that her mother was traveling for her new job, but she missed her.

On the curb, Kathy tripped on her shoelace. As she bent over to tie it, she remembered her fourth birthday, when Gram had given her white tap shoes with ribbon ties. Gram's eyes had lit up when Kathy put them on. But when Kathy had tried to shuffle across the kitchen floor, she slipped and fell. Her grandma had looked disappointed.

Kathy sighed deeply. That awkward fall had happened seven years ago, and she had never put on tap shoes since.

She could see her dog, Snuggles, with his nose pressed against the car window. She ran over and jumped in beside him. "I brought you a treat," she said, holding out a fry.

Snuggles gobbled it down and looked up for more.

"I've really missed you," she said, rubbing his fluffy white head. "At least we won't have to worry about you chasing a cat at Gram's house. She doesn't have one."

Kathy's dad hesitated with his hand on the door. "Bad news, honey. Grandma's allergies have flared up, so Snuggles can't go with you."

"I can't believe this," Kathy protested. Snuggles couldn't come with her to Aunt Sharon's, either, because of her cat.

"I'm sorry. I know it doesn't seem fair," he said. "But school will be starting soon and then Snuggles will be sleeping next to you every night." He studied her face and shook his head. "Hard to believe. A few weeks and you'll be in sixth grade. Soon—too soon."

Kathy frowned and kissed Snuggles on the top of his small black nose. *Soon,* she thought. Parents always said "soon." Soon to them seemed like forever to her. But, she had to admit, the time spent at Riversend with her aunt hadn't seemed very long. Even though she had missed Snuggles, when her dad came to pick her up, she cried.

"There's Monterey Bay," her dad said, pointing straight ahead. "Look at the sand dunes and the seagulls. You'll have a great time here."

"Alone?" she asked wistfully. "Gram's neighbors don't have any kids, you know."

"You made friends at Riversend," her dad said. "There's no reason why you can't again. Monterey could be another adventure for you."

Kathy hoped her dad was right. She loved her Grandma Bev. As far back as she could remember, her visits to Monterey had always been on weekends and holidays, and her parents had been along. Mostly they spent time together at the beach or on the pier with all the little shops and restaurants. Sometimes she went with her mother and Gram to the town of Carmel to shop in boutiques. And of course she couldn't forget the times spent at the Monterey Aquarium.

Lots to do, she told herself, but this time she'd be alone.

She gazed out over the horizon and focused on a rim of gray where the sea met the sky. Fog! She hated it. A sudden panic grabbed her. What if it was foggy every day and she had to stay in the house to entertain Gram while her knee mended? Kathy slumped down in her seat. She hoped Gram watched lots of TV.

A few miles later, her dad turned off the Pacific Coast Highway and entered the town of Monterey. Soon he pulled up in front of a small two-story cottage painted bright pink with white gingerbread trim. Large purple and white flowers spilled over a picket fence that surrounded a tiny garden, making the whole place look like something out of a fairy tale.

Kathy stood on the wooden porch next to her dad while he rapped first, then opened the door. "Mom, it's Dan—and Kathy."

"Come on in," a stuffed-up voice called from somewhere at the rear of the house. From down the hall came a shuffling noise. Gram appeared around the corner wearing bright blue stretch pants with an Ace bandage covering one knee and a gold sweatshirt with GOTTA DANCE across the front in black letters. She stopped and leaned on a cane while she dabbed at her red nose with a handkerchief.

Kathy was surprised to see her grandma limping. Gram, a tall blond dancer and teacher, always stood straight and moved gracefully.

Bev Wicklow leaned against the wall while she held out her arms. "Come here, you two. Give me a hug." She tapped her fingers on the head of the cane as Kathy walked over. "Don't let this old thing scare you. It's only temporary, believe me." She glanced confidently at Kathy's dad and her blue eyes sparkled. "I'll be back on my toes before long. But in the meantime, it will be nice to have you here, Kathy. Aunt Sharon called to tell me about your stay up in the gold country. Sounds like you had quite a time."

11

"Uh huh," Kathy agreed with a grunt as her grandmother gave her a squeeze. "A great time."

"Remember the times we used to have there, Dan?" Gram said in a teasing voice. "When you were small, you never wanted to go up to the country. And then when it was time to leave, you sulked all the way home."

Kathy looked at her dad with wonder, trying to picture him as a sulky kid.

"What's all this?" her dad asked, obviously trying to change the subject. He pointed to a round card table and chairs arranged in the living room. "Are you expecting company?"

Kathy thought she saw her grandma blush. "A friend set this up. Some people I know are coming over this evening." Then it seemed like she hurried to change the subject. "Tell me all about you, Dan. And how is Diane's new job working out?" Gram looked at Kathy. "I'm disappointed that your mom had to work today. I know she must be very busy."

Gram and Kathy's father started talking about family matters, so Kathy went out to the car and brought in her things, taking them directly upstairs to the loft bedroom where she always stayed. The loft had a slanted ceiling and it was all done in yellow—curtains, quilted bedspread, and little buttercups on the wallpaper.

To her left was the door to a walk-in closet. On

the far wall, a window faced west, where she could look out and see the bay. She unpacked her art pad and pencils and set them on the dresser. If she had to stay in the house and keep Gram company, then she'd have plenty of time to draw.

Whistling softly, she went to the window. The fog, gray and wispy, moved in from the ocean. As she watched, something happened. Some of the mist seemed to gather and take shape. A shiver passed through her as the odd form moved toward the shore, then spread out.

She turned and patted the top of the patchwork quilt. This might be a good night to get under the covers and read her new mystery novel. Before leaving, she went back to the window. The fog had thinned. With a sigh of relief, she rushed from the loft and bounded down the steps to see what her dad and Gram were up to.

"Don't worry about dinner," she heard her grandmother saying. "My friend Loretta owns a Spanish restaurant in town. She's coming over tonight and she's bringing food." Gram sat in a high-back chair and motioned for Kathy. "Just wait till you meet Loretta's granddaughter and grandnephew. They're great kids. I've told them all about you."

"Are they coming tonight, too?" Kathy asked, feeling shy but excited.

"No," her grandmother said. Her voice sounded

stiff and strange. "Not tonight." She hesitated a moment, then gave Kathy a broad smile. "But you'll meet them tomorrow. I promise." Gram looked over at Kathy's dad and blushed again. "This is a special meeting tonight. Definitely not for children."

CHAPTER
2

Tacos and burritos and salsa! Kathy had been in heaven at dinnertime. Gram's friend Loretta, a chubby woman with salt-and-pepper hair, sure knew how to cook. After dinner Kathy's dad left the cottage to drive back home. Not long after that, Gram hustled Kathy up to bed, saying that they had a big day tomorrow and that she should get her sleep. Loretta, glancing around nervously, had agreed, then invited Kathy over to her restaurant for lunch tomorrow to meet her family.

Now, up in the loft, as Kathy cuddled under the covers with her book, she heard the doorbell ring. When Gram opened the front door, a man's voice drifted up. Kathy could understand why she had to go to bed early. But why hadn't she been allowed to stay up and meet Gram's other friend? Gram had acted so mysterious about this meeting tonight.

Kathy crossed her arms and drummed her fingers on her elbow. Gram lived alone. Could this guy be her boyfriend? Was she embarrassed for Kathy to know?

Her curiosity kept her thoughts spinning. She sighed and closed her book. Each time she read a paragraph, she had to go back and reread it. At this speed it would take her all night to get through a chapter.

She switched off the light and scrunched down under the quilt, but no matter how hard she tried, she couldn't go to sleep. The voices from downstairs kept her awake. A little while later the talking stopped. She couldn't sleep then because it was too quiet. After tossing around on the bed, she got up, slipped through the door, and sat on the top step. The rooms downstairs were dark except for a dim glow that came from the living room. All was quiet. Where did everyone go?

She moved down two steps. No sound. Six more steps brought her down far enough to see under the arch separating the hall entrance from the living room. Wow! At least a dozen lit candles flickered on tables and shelves around the room.

In the middle of the round card table, a big white

candle lit up the faces of the three adults—Gram, Loretta, and a bearded stranger. Shadows danced eerily across their closed eyes as they sat at the table holding hands.

The muted light made it difficult for Kathy to see, and she leaned forward to peer through the banister. What were they doing? Praying? Meditating? Then, quite suddenly, Loretta began to speak. Kathy drew back and pressed against the wall.

"Ramón. Oh, Ramón," she pleaded in a drawn-out voice. "Can you hear me? I need your help. Please, speak to me—give me a sign—direct me to the deed."

Silence again. Silence except for the sound of the man's breathing. Kathy thought she saw Gram's eyelids flutter. She did see the man open his eyes, glance around at the others, then, spotting Kathy on the staircase, stare right at her.

She turned to crawl back up the steps when she smelled a strong whiff of salt. She wrinkled her nose. Over by the window, behind the man, she could see fog creeping up to the glass. It spread out in a thin layer, then slid through the crack under the windowsill. In the room, it gathered in on itself, thickening, flowing into a gray form.

Kathy forgot about the man's staring eyes as she watched the fog swirl around Loretta's head, rise to the ceiling, and settle in a corner. Did anyone else see it? Probably not. Loretta still called for Ramón. Gram's eyes remained shut, and the man still stared at Kathy. The eerie shape stayed up in the corner for a few moments before it floated down toward the table.

While Kathy pondered the strange situation, a misty shape like a finger poked out from the gray fog and wavered in front of Loretta, who couldn't see it because her eyes were squeezed shut.

Click! The room immediately flooded with light. Kathy had been so preoccupied with the fog that she hadn't seen Gram reach for the switch. Gram stood and limped over to Loretta to console her. Kathy hurried up to her room and jumped into bed. A few seconds later, she got up and went over to the window. The night was clear—stars glittered in the dark sky. The billowing fog she had seen earlier had retreated.

The sound of the front door opening and closing caught her attention and she looked down. The stranger, with his broad-brimmed hat pulled over his eyes, walked away from the porch. He opened the gate, stood next to the street lamp in a circle of light, and looked up at her. Then he tipped his hat.

"Whoa, he knows I'm watching him," Kathy cried, jumping back into bed. "And that guy doesn't like it—or me."

"What makes you think Mr. Mason dislikes you?" Gram asked the next morning. "He doesn't even know you."

Kathy poured herself a glass of milk and joined her grandma at the kitchen table. "He looked up at my window with mean eyes when he was leaving last night. And how come you didn't let me meet him?"

"I don't know why you were awake so late," Gram said, handing Kathy a napkin. "And you didn't meet him because he isn't a social person. He doesn't like to be around people."

Kathy sipped at her milk. "You and Loretta are people."

"He's Loretta's boarder. He lives above the restaurant. The only reason he comes here is because he's trying to help Loretta. And," Gram muttered, "to help himself, I'm sure."

"Help her? How?"

Gram poured a drop of cream in her tea and stirred it thoughtfully. "It's financial business, Kathy. I don't think you would be interested."

"Why do you do financial business by candle-light?"

Gram looked surprised. "Were you spying on us?"

Kathy squinted and made a face. "Yep. Awful, huh? I couldn't sleep and I heard the doorbell ring and I wondered who it was. So I peeked." She spread a daub of blueberry jam across her toast. "When I go over to Loretta's place for lunch, will Mr. Mason be there? Are you coming with me? Is she going to pick us up?"

"Hold it!" Gram laughed and raised her hand. "One question at a time. I am going with you. Loretta is picking us up," she said, then, more to herself than to Kathy, "and it's hard to tell where Mason will be."

"Gram," Kathy said. "I saw something last night. Something strange."

Gram looked up quickly. "Where? When?"

"In the living room. When you were doing financial business."

"What did you see?"

Kathy thought a moment. "While Loretta was calling for Ramón—who is Ramón anyway?"

"Her husband," Gram said impatiently. "Go on."

"Where was he?"

"Nowhere. He's dead."

Kathy's mouth dropped open.

"Kathy, please get on with it."

"Well, there was this fog. It came in under the window and went up to the ceiling."

"Oh, is that all?" Gram said with relief. "Sometimes in these old houses, mists settle in."

"But Gram," Kathy said, shaking her head.

"First there was this strong salty smell." She pinched her nose. "Then the mist had a finger, and it pointed at Loretta."

Gram peered at Kathy over the rim of her cup. "Imagination is a wonderful, creative power, my dear girl. But sometimes we have to be careful when we use it. It can play tricks on us."

Tricks, nicks, Kathy thought. She knew what she had seen, and if Gram and her friends had another one of their financial meetings, she would sit on the stairs again and watch for that creepy fog.

CHAPTER
3

"La Costa," Gram explained to Kathy on their drive over to Loretta's restaurant, "means 'coast' in Spanish. Right, Loretta?"

Loretta nodded. "This restaurant, La Costa, was built a long time ago. A hundred years after one of my ancestors, a Spanish soldier stationed at the presidio in Monterey, married an Indian woman in 1775. He decided to stay here and was given a land grant of thirty thousand acres by the king of Spain." Loretta glanced back at Kathy with a proud smile. "My roots go back to the early days when Monterey was ruled by Spain, when cattle roamed huge ranchos, and their owners, the rancheros, were aristocrats."

Loretta gestured. "This town was the military and social capital of California then."

Kathy's eyes widened. "You own thirty thousand acres? You must be rich!"

"Not me," Loretta replied with a bitter laugh. "The plot where La Costa stands now is all that's left of the land once known as El Rancho del Encina, the Oak Ranch."

"What happened to all of it?" Kathy asked.

"It's a long story. In order to answer your question, I'll have to tell you a little of Monterey history." Loretta took a deep breath. "Three nations have flown their flags over Monterey—Spain, Mexico, and the United States. But the Indians were here first. Some of them were my ancestors, too. They lived in their own villages—villages the Spanish called *rancherias.*"

Loretta stopped at an intersection, looked both ways, then drove on. "A very long time ago," she continued, "Mexico—which included California—was controlled by Spain. Spanish padres—the priests—were sent to build missions in Mexico and California and convert the Indians to Christianity. Spanish soldiers were ordered to build presidios—forts to protect the missions—using Indians as slave labor. That's why my soldier ancestor was sent here.

"But Mexico, wanting its own rule, fought Spain

for many years and finally won its independence in 1822. Then California became part of Mexico. Later, in 1846, the Americans took California from the Mexicans. The Rancho del Encina belonged to my family for over a hundred years until the land was taken away by the Americans. Squatters, they called themselves."

Kathy looked puzzled. "Squatters?"

Loretta nodded. "Americans who came here to settle. They found plenty of land with roaming cattle and decided to take the land and build on it."

"That's stealing," Kathy said, looking first at Loretta then at her grandmother.

"That's right." Gram nodded at Loretta. "The *Californios*...that's what the early people who lived here then, who mostly spoke Spanish, called themselves. Well, the Californios couldn't understand English and knew little about American laws. When the squatters went to court to lay claim to the property, the courts gave the Californios two years to produce papers proving the land was theirs."

"And," Loretta added, "the majority of the land-grant boundaries were marked by rivers, boulders, or trees. Sometimes papers couldn't be found." She glanced at Kathy's grandmother. "Looks like history is repeating itself."

"Except," Gram said with a hopeful lilt to her

voice, "you know that somewhere—someplace—there is a Spanish deed for La Costa."

"But where?" Loretta sighed. She pulled the car up to the curb. "Enough history for today. Let's have lunch."

She got out of the car and moved to the curb to help Bev. "We pride ourselves here at La Costa in serving authentic Spanish-Indian food as well as the popular Mexican food you're probably used to, Kathy."

Kathy jumped out of the car. Loretta's place was spectacular. Bright green bushes that looked like miniature palm trees flanked the red brick walkway. Two wrought-iron wall lamps hung on both sides of the front door. Above the door was a stained glass window shaped like a half-moon.

The front door of the restaurant flew open and two kids raced down the steps. Kathy turned just in time to see a pretty, dark-haired girl in pink shorts and a skinny boy wearing glasses.

"Yay! Beat you," said the boy, making a face.

"You little brat," the girl said, looking down at him. "Why do you always have to be first?"

"I don't have to be," he said smugly. "I just am!"

"Okay, you two," Loretta said, reaching for their hands and pulling them close. "I want you to meet Bev's granddaughter. Kathy, this is Lisa, my granddaughter, and Dennis, my grandnephew."

"She's eleven and I'm nine," Dennis said, standing as tall as he could. "And don't call me Dennis. I'm Digger!"

"Hi," Lisa said.

Kathy immediately liked this pretty girl with her smiling brown eyes. She reminded Kathy of Robyn, her best friend at school.

"And hi, Teach," Lisa said to Gram. "I've been practicing every day on those riff steps you taught our class." She stepped onto her left foot. Then she raised her right foot off the sidewalk and hit her toe on the cement before sliding her foot forward and scuffing her heel. She laughed. "When I bus tables at lunch, I riff around the room."

Everyone except Digger laughed with her. "Do you dance?" Lisa asked Kathy. "You must. Your grandma teaches."

"Nope. I don't," Kathy said, avoiding her grandmother's eyes. "Gram has tried—but..."

"That's okay," Lisa said. "I'll help you. Then you can be in the pageant."

"Pageant? What's that?"

"A spectacular display," Digger stated.

Lisa glanced uncertainly at Digger then nodded. "It's that too. But it's more like a musical play put on for Hispanic Heritage Month."

"Depicting the early history of Monterey," Loretta added. "There will be singing and dancing, and costumes and scenery portraying the Indian, Spanish, and American Californios. All those early people we talked about in the car." She gave Bev a pat on the back. "Your grandma has done the choreography. Now she'll be directing the dancers at rehearsals."

They all started for the door of the restaurant. As Gram eased her way up the front steps, Kathy looked up. Directly above her in a window that jutted out over the sidewalk, Mr. Mason stood staring down.

Lisa saw Kathy look up and she did too. "That's our boarder."

"I know," Kathy replied. "What's his problem?"

"Problem?"

Kathy shuddered. "He stares—and he's creepy."

"You think he's creepy?"

"Well, weird, anyway."

"He's not," Digger said, overhearing them. "He's a good guy. He knows a lot about a lot of stuff."

"Why does he stare like that?" Kathy said softly so Digger wouldn't hear.

Lisa moved closer. "I don't know. He always does. Guess I'm used to it."

"Aunt Loretta," Digger called out. "They're saying bad things about Mr. Mason. Make them stop."

Loretta waggled a finger at Lisa then went right back to her discussion with Bev. When they got inside, Kathy gasped. "This place is beautiful." She wandered around, looking at the red-and-white wallpaper that covered the top half of the dark wood walls, and at the polished brass cash register that sat on the counter. "This house is old, huh?"

"Late 1800s," Loretta said proudly.

To the right stood a staircase that led up to an open indoor balcony with a banister and a glass-domed ceiling. "Is that where he lives?" Kathy asked Lisa.

"Yep," Lisa said. "The room to the right. Sometimes I look up and he's staring down from that rotunda."

"A rotunda means round," Digger said. "That hallway up there is round and it has a dome. A rotunda."

Lisa gave an irritated sigh. "Do you carry a dictionary in your pocket?"

"Nope," Digger said. "The dictionary's up here." He pointed to his head.

Lisa looked at Kathy. "He's too much. Smart though, the little brat. I guess Mason teaches him a lot of stuff."

They all ate in the big kitchen in the back. "This is an early lunch," Loretta said to Kathy as she served the salads. "We usually eat before the restaurant opens."

"Do you all live here?" Kathy asked.

"We stay in Grandma's house out back," said Lisa. She pointed out the window. "Behind the patio, past those tables. We've been here all summer."

"I'm moving in here," said Digger. "I'm going to stay with Mason."

"In your dreams!" said Lisa.

Digger picked at his food. "Well, I want to, anyway."

He looked so sad that Kathy felt sorry for him. "You really like this guy, huh?"

Digger nodded. "He's the only man around here. Except for me. He lets me work with him while he builds his ship in a bottle. He lets me touch his gun collection—and he reads to me about pirates."

Kathy noticed Gram give Loretta a questioning look. "You let Dennis touch Mason's guns? Is that safe?"

Loretta shrugged. "When Digger first told me, I got angry. Angry that Mason would bring those guns into La Costa. But after Mason showed me his collection and explained that the pins had been removed, I gave my permission. He likes the boy and the boy adores him. Why not?"

Lisa poked Kathy's arm. "I think he's an old pirate."

CHAPTER
4

"Do you really believe Mr. Mason is a pirate?" Kathy asked later when they were in Lisa's room. She walked to the open window and looked out at the bay. "You think he's a shipjacker?"

Lisa opened her closet and took out three sequined tap costumes and held them up. "I bet we wear the same size. Do you want to try one on?"

"I don't think so. Remember? I don't dance."

"You don't have to tap or wear any of these to be in the pageant," Lisa said, spreading two of the costumes out on the bed. "You just have to learn a few slow, Indian-type dance steps. And wear feathers." She turned around abruptly. "You do have rhythm, don't you?"

Kathy shrugged. "I'm not sure. I want to know more about Mr. Mason. You called him a pirate."

Lisa held the red-and-white tap costume up to her own shoulders as she posed in front of the mirror. "I was only joking. I have to bus his table every day when he's through eating lunch. He's messy. He reads while he eats and drops papers and napkins on the floor and never bothers to pick them up. He litters. And I hate litterers!"

Kathy moved over and spoke to Lisa's reflection in the mirror. "Do you think he's weird?"

Lisa wrinkled her nose. "Kind of. But he doesn't bother me. And don't mention that I called him a pirate. If Digger finds out, he'll tell him."

Lisa gathered up her costumes and went to the closet. Kathy sat down on the edge of the bed. "Lisa. What kind of financial business do our grandmas do—by candlelight?"

Lisa twirled around, her eyes wide. "Did you see them? Tell me about it. They never have their meetings here. My grandma and Mason always go over to your Grandma Bev's."

Kathy told Lisa about what she had seen the night before. "I don't know what that mist—or fog—or whatever—was. I just know that it looked really weird, and I could tell Mason doesn't like me."

Lisa plopped down next to Kathy. "I heard my

mom say they're doing a seance. My grandma is hunting for some papers and your Gram is helping her."

Kathy thought a moment. "Your grandma kept calling for Ramón."

"I know. Ramón's my grandpa that died," Lisa said, looking sad. "Grandma's really stressed. I heard her tell Mason that there's some dispute about La Costa's land title. A cloud over it, whatever that means. She said my grandpa stopped paying taxes on the property a long time ago. And that our family's going to lose this property unless we can find the original Spanish grant to prove the land is ours. Grandma believes Ramón can tell her where it is."

Kathy looked shocked. "Lose this property? This is all that's left from your family's ranch."

Lisa nodded. "I know. Isn't it awful?"

"What's Mason got to do with it? During the seance while Loretta and Gram kept their eyes shut, his were open."

"He's writing a history book. My grandma says he goes there in case some spirits are floating around. He thinks they might give him some historical facts for his book."

"Does your mom ever do the seance with them?"

"No way! She's in San Francisco going to law school. She thinks they're all nuts."

"Do you?"

"I'm not sure," Lisa said. After a moment Lisa asked, "What did your grandma say when you told her about the fog?"

"She thinks it's my imagination."

"Are you sure it isn't?"

"Yes, I'm sure." Kathy waited for Lisa to say something, but Lisa just sat there looking doubtful.

Gram didn't believe her and now Lisa didn't either. Kathy got up to go back to the restaurant when a scraping noise from under the window made both girls look over. Lisa jumped up and went to the window. Kathy followed. Digger was outside, kneeling on the ground with a forked tool in one hand and a magnifying glass in the other.

"What's he doing?" Kathy asked.

Digger glanced up, then immediately returned to his work. The girls watched him burrow and scrape until finally he dropped the forked tool, jumped to his feet, and held up a long thin rock. "It's a Cynodont," he shouted.

Kathy looked at Lisa.

"He thinks he's found another fossil," Lisa said. "That's why he's Digger. He's a dinosaur-fossil-freak."

Kathy leaned out the window. "Can I see it—hold it?" She reached out her hand.

Digger stepped back and clutched the rock in

his fist. "It's not a dinosaur," he said excitedly. "Cynodonts were mammal-like reptiles. They were here. Way before the dinosaurs."

"Digger. Just let me feel it," Kathy said.

"No," he said, snapping his hand away.

"Why? I won't take it. I just want to look at it." Digger took off his glasses.

"He can't see you now," Lisa said. "That's why he takes them off. So he won't have to talk to you."

Digger fumbled around on the ground until he found the forked tool. With both hands full, he turned to go.

Lisa's eyes narrowed. "How long have you been out there, Digger?"

Digger didn't answer. He kept moving toward the restaurant.

"Digger! I'm warning you," Lisa said. "If you heard anything we said in here..."

Digger turned around and squinted.

Lisa put one leg over the sill, threatening to jump out. "You tell Mason one word and I'll strangle you."

Digger took off at a trot and made his way across the patio, bumping into tables and scattering metal chairs. When he reached the door to the kitchen, he turned around, dug in his pocket for his glasses, and slipped them into place. "You're both in trouble now," he called. "I'm going upstairs."

34

There was a rap at the door. Kathy's grandma peeked in.

"I'm going home now," she said. "If you want, you can stay."

"I'd like to," Kathy said. "But it's a long walk home—alone."

Lisa held her lips tight, but she couldn't stop the smile that was forming.

"What?" Kathy looked at Gram. Gram smiled at Lisa, then they both started to laugh.

"Come on," her grandma motioned. "Come outside."

They walked out on the porch. Pointing her cane dramatically, Gram motioned to the corner of the house. Loretta peeked around. She held the handlebars of a shiny, brand-new orange-and-silver bike.

Kathy gasped. "It's beautiful!"

Gram took Kathy's hand. "And it's yours."

Kathy ran to Loretta and wheeled the bike out. Then she tried it for size. "The seat's just right," she said with delight. "This is just what I wanted."

Gram nodded. "I'm glad."

From the upstairs window overlooking the patio, Digger hollered down to Kathy and Lisa. "I told Mason what you said about him and you both better watch out." He leaned over too far and had to catch himself. While he struggled to pull himself back in, the girls looked at each other and giggled.

Digger pointed his fossil at them menacingly. "You guys have had it!"

Above Digger's head, Kathy saw Mason's staring eyes.

And above Mason floated the ghostly gray fog.

CHAPTER
5

"Did you see that?" Kathy asked Lisa as they climbed on their bikes.

"Yeah," Lisa said. "Mason was staring again."

"No," Kathy insisted. "I mean the fog."

Lisa looked confused. "Where?"

"Up in the window," Kathy said. "Above Mason's head."

"Fog? I only saw Digger and Mason." Lisa gave the bike pedal a push and headed out front. "There's no fog today," she called back. "You must have been seeing things."

Kathy followed and caught up. "I know. I do see things—and where are we going?"

Lisa looked straight ahead. "For a ride."

"How about the beach?" Kathy suggested. "Let's go down to the water. I want to see if there's fog out there."

"I can't today," Lisa said, sounding unfriendly. "There's too many dark clouds moving in. Without the sun the sand will be cold."

"The clouds aren't that dark," Kathy persisted.

Lisa didn't reply. She pedaled faster.

The girls rode along in silence until Kathy spoke. "What's wrong, Lisa? You act mad."

Lisa slowed down, then stopped. "It's this fog thing. I don't know what you're talking about."

"That's because you're not listening." Kathy felt the heat rise to her face. "I hate fog. And it's no fun to see something you hate when no one else does—and no one believes you. But I need to believe that what I'm seeing is okay. I kind of did last night."

"How come?"

"Someone—one of my ancestors, a very beautiful aunt—let me know that it was a gift to see things that others don't."

"A gift? Sounds more like a curse."

Kathy frowned. She took a deep breath. "Last night at the cottage when the fog seeped in, I was curious. I wondered why it was there and what it was doing."

"Nothing," Lisa said irritably. "Fog doesn't *do*

anything. It just is. Stop worrying about it. Forget it."

Kathy started to ride again. She decided not to mention the fog to Lisa ever again. Unless, of course, she had to.

"You'll see Mason pretty soon," Lisa called after her in a warning tone. "He'll be down for lunch. That's another reason why I can't go to the beach. I have to help my grandma serve and clean up."

After four blocks of energetic riding, with no more talk of the fog or Mason, the girls made a U-turn and went back to La Costa. In the kitchen, Lisa handed Kathy an apron. "Want to help?"

Kathy grinned and nodded. "Sure. It sounds fun. Tell me what to do."

"Fun for you, maybe," Lisa said. "But I've been doing this all summer. It gets boring."

"All summer? Where's your dad? Do you have any sisters or brothers?"

Lisa wrapped the strings of her apron around her waist and tied them in front. "I've got one brother. He's seventeen. His name's Ruben and he's a junior this year and he models at an agency in San Francisco." Lisa rolled her eyes. "He's so handsome. He wants to be an actor." She crossed to a drawer under the cabinets, rummaged around in it, and pulled out a big glossy picture. "Isn't he great?"

Kathy had to agree. "He's awesome!" After studying the picture, she handed it back to Lisa. "Does he live with your mom in the city?"

"Nope. With my dad." She carefully replaced the picture in the drawer. "My parents are divorced. That's why my mom's in law school. She's thirty-eight and she says she's getting old. She wants to be a success before it's too late." Lisa looked sad.

"Guess you miss her, huh?"

Lisa nodded. "I miss my dad and Ruben too. They're both really neat. But San Francisco's not that far away. Everyone's so busy, though, I don't get to see them that often. When my mother finishes school, she's moving back here." Lisa checked the clock on the wall. "Yikes. My grandma will be in soon. We better get busy."

Kathy went to the swinging door and peeked out. The dining room was empty. "Who waits on Mason? You?"

"Not if I can help it," Lisa said. "Today you can do it."

"He doesn't like me," Kathy said. "He might ask me about last night."

"Don't worry, he never talks," said Lisa, spreading plates out on the big table in the center of the kitchen. "He just stares. Half the time I don't think he knows what he's staring at." She counted the plates, then glanced at Kathy. "You'll hear him when he comes down. He always comes early and clomps on those stairs like he's trying to break them."

Lisa had no sooner spoken than the clomps began.

"I told you," Lisa said loudly.

"Told her what?" Loretta asked, coming in from outside, her arms filled with grocery bags. "And why are you yelling?"

Lisa looked flustered. "I told Kathy she could wait on tables," she stammered.

"Is that okay, Loretta?" Kathy asked, feeling flustered along with Lisa without knowing why.

"*Puedo contar con usted?*" Loretta asked Kathy with a wink as she removed heads of lettuce from the bags.

Kathy looked surprised, smiled shyly, and shrugged. As Loretta passed Kathy, she gave her a pat on the shoulder.

Lisa laughed. "Grandma asked if she can count on you. If you hang around here, you'll learn some Spanish."

"A pair of extra hands will help today," Loretta said. "And you'll get paid what Lisa does—plus tips."

Kathy could hardly contain her delight. A fun job. And she was getting paid. She tied the strings of her apron tighter and adjusted the bib.

41

Loretta handed Kathy a salad and bowed from the waist like a head waiter. "Here you go, *señorita.* Mr. Mason awaits."

Kathy looked down at the plate then over at Lisa. Lisa grinned and rolled her eyes.

Loretta pushed open the door and gently nudged Kathy through. Mason was alone out front. He sat at a table reading a newspaper. When Kathy stepped out, he didn't bother to look up, so she had time to study him.

His hair and eyebrows were jet black and his eyes were just as dark. Beneath his graying beard he wore a faded red scarf tied loosely around his neck. When he reached for his glass of water, Kathy could see that the little finger of his right hand was missing above the middle joint.

Kathy hesitated a moment, then moved silently across the hardwood floor toward Mason's table. Mason eyed Kathy as he let the paper slide down through his thick fingers. Kathy placed the salad in front of him and turned quickly to leave.

"Wait," Mason said. "Come back here."

Kathy didn't turn around, but she didn't move on either.

"Did you hear me, girl?" His gravelly voice seemed to have an accent. What kind? Kathy couldn't tell.

She summoned her courage and turned around.

Mason glared at her and Kathy stared back. He pointed at the white tablecloth. "I gave you an order!"

Kathy took a deep breath. "I don't take orders from strangers," she said in a hardy tone, surprising herself.

Mason leaned back against the chair. "So you've got spunk, have you?" He gave a wheezy laugh.

Kathy ran back to the kitchen. When she reached the other side of the swinging door, she leaned against the wall and let out a huge sigh of relief. "He's scary," she said, looking from Lisa to Loretta.

"What did he do?" Lisa asked. "Spill his salad?"

"Nope. He tried to order me around."

"You two." Loretta shook her head. "That's what customers do. They give the waitress an order. He just wants his soup. I'll serve him. You both get busy with the salads."

"Tell me what he said," Lisa whispered after her grandma left the kitchen. "He always ignores me."

"It's not what he said, exactly," Kathy said, making a face. "It's the way he said it—his voice."

"I like his voice," Digger said, springing out from behind a cupboard.

Kathy jumped and Lisa caught her breath.

"He sings to me sometimes," Digger continued. "Old songs about the sea." He started to hum.

43

"Stop it, Digger," Lisa warned. "One of these times you're going to get hurt when you pop up out of nowhere."

Digger and Lisa started arguing, but Kathy wasn't listening. That tune Digger hummed. She'd heard it before. But where?

CHAPTER

6

When lunch was over at the restaurant, Kathy rode her bike back to the cottage. "Guess what, Gram," she called, bursting into the living room. "I waited tables at La Costa."

Gram put her book down and smiled. "Great! Good experience for you."

"And I got paid," Kathy said, strutting around the living room. "I made four dollars."

Gram gave two approving taps of her cane. "Wonderful."

Kathy sat down in a chair and grinned. "I put my new bike away in the garage. Is that okay?"

"Fine. That's a safe place. How was the ride?"

Kathy threw her arms in the air. "It goes fast

like the wind. Thanks. I love it." She jumped up, rushed over to Gram, and gave her a big hug.

On the ride home from La Costa, Kathy had decided she really wanted to be in the pageant with Lisa. After listening to Loretta's story about her family and California history, Kathy wanted to be part of it. Even for just one night. She planned to surprise Gram, but the thought of learning to dance made her stomach clutch.

She removed herself from Gram's arms and went over to the bookcase. The whole second shelf bulged with books on dancing. She pulled one out and looked at the cover. A man and a woman held their arms out while they pointed their toes and kicked high. Kathy leaned back, tried to copy them, and bumped up against the bookcase, knocking over a small crystal bell.

"You all right?" Gram asked, glancing over her shoulder.

Kathy blushed. "Yep. Nothing broke. Just looking for a book to read. Guess I lost my balance." She smiled sheepishly as she set the bell upright on the shelf. "I'm so clumsy."

"It might be better if you concentrated on the balance part, Kathy, and forgot about the 'clumsy.' I believe that what we think or say about ourselves is important." She sniffed and dabbed at her nose with a hanky. "Don't you?"

Kathy thought a moment. "You mean if I stop saying I'm clumsy, I won't be?"

"Might take some time, but it's worth a try."

Kathy nodded and slipped the book under her T-shirt. "I do—I do—I do have balance," she chanted uncertainly as she strode down the hall toward the back door. "I'll be out on the deck," she called to Gram as the door closed behind her.

The small wooden deck framed with a railing seemed to be the perfect place for her to practice. First she would try to learn the steps here on the wooden planks in her tennis shoes. Then, if Lisa would let her borrow her tap shoes, she'd give it a try on the floor in Lisa's room.

She studied the practice routine in the book, propped it up in the corner of the deck, then held on to the rail. Carefully following the instructions for Lesson 1, she straightened her spine, held her free arm out to the side, and tried not to arch her back.

She did a front brush, a side brush, and a back brush. Sixteen times with her right foot, then sixteen times with her left. That wasn't too hard. Her knuckles were white from gripping the railing. What would happen when she wore slippery tap shoes and had only her hips to hang on to?

She sighed, reached over, and gathered up the book. Enough for today.

47

Inside, she whistled cheerfully as she wandered down the hall. Gram was still reading. Kathy slipped the book back on the shelf, then turned around and spotted the music box on the fireplace mantle. She remembered Digger's song, the one Mason had taught him.

"Gram," she said. "Where did you get this music box?"

Gram looked up. "Loretta," she said thoughtfully. "She gave me that a long time ago—Christmas, I think. Or maybe my birthday. We've been friends for years. When you were a baby, I used to play it for you when you came to visit. You got so excited then." She motioned toward the box. "I believe it's wound. Open the lid."

Kathy did, and the music instantly spilled out, a lively little tune that played over and over. "What kind of music is it?" Kathy asked, running her hand over the small wooden box, which was painted like an old chest.

"Loretta said it's an old, old tune that dates back to the early days of California. Could be music from a number of different cultures—Indian, Spanish, or Mexican. Loretta found it in an antique store somewhere up in the Carmel Valley."

"Digger knows this song," Kathy said, sitting down on the stone hearth. "He was humming it in Loretta's kitchen."

Gram smiled. "He's such a darling child," she said. "I've seen how he moves when they play music at La Costa. He's a natural. Too bad I can't give him a few private lessons, teach him a couple of steps before he goes back home to New Mexico. If I weren't laid up..."

She shook her cane in protest.

"Dennis would have been perfect for the pageant," she added. "But he didn't want to perform." She gazed out the window. "I know exactly where I would have placed him, too. In the chorus of children, all descendants of the Costanoans."

Kathy felt uncomfortable. Lisa could dance—Digger was a natural. It seemed like everyone had talent except her. "What's a Costanoan?" she asked.

"Coast Indians," Gram explained.

The music box was running down, giving the lively melody a haunting sound. "Loretta's ancestor, the Indian woman who married the Spanish soldier, must have been a Costanoan, huh?"

"That's right," Gram replied. "Loretta's roots in this country go way back. Mr. Mason is a historian. He's doing research on Loretta's ancestors, and he says that the Costanoans settled in this area around 500 B.C."

"Whoa! That's over two thousand years ago. This peninsula must have looked a lot different then."

Gram pointed to the bookcase. "That blue book on the third shelf. *Early American Indians.* Could you bring it here, please?"

Kathy gave her the book.

After checking the index, Gram riffled the pages. "This is a picture an artist did of the Costanoans—much later on, when they first sighted a ship in Monterey Bay."

Kathy sat on the arm of the chair and looked at the book. Two Indian men, naked except for moccasins and two feathers stuck in the back of their hair, peered over a boulder at a ship rigged with four sails.

She read the bold print below the picture: "Weather permitting, the natives went naked. Men coated themselves with mud on cold mornings until the warming sun caused it to drop off. They lived on plants, roots, shellfish, and small game. They were excellent marksmen."

Her eyes darted back to the picture. She remembered Lisa telling her about the feather costumes. "Gram," she said, alarmed. "Are the kids in the pageant going to wear just moccasins and a couple of feathers?"

Gram laughed. "No, no. They'll wear more. The boys will wear buckskin and the girls will wear short skirts made of bark fiber. We're trying to keep the clothes as authentic as we can."

Relieved, Kathy wound the music box again. "Digger said Mr. Mason taught him this song. How does he know it?"

"I don't know. Maybe Loretta sings it around the restaurant. The next time you see Mr. Mason, you could ask him."

Kathy shook her head. "No way. I'm never going to ask him anything."

"Still feel he doesn't like you?"

"I know he doesn't," Kathy said. "I waited on him at lunch. Weird—weird—weirdo!"

"Did he speak to you?" Gram asked.

Kathy stood and folded her arms tightly across her chest. "Yep. And he's rude. He tried to order me around."

Gram's eyes were alert. "Order? How?"

"Real rude. He had a low voice and he ordered me back to his table."

Gram frowned. "What did you do?"

"I just marched back to the kitchen."

Gram reached out. "Come here, Kathy."

Kathy went over to her, and Gram squeezed her hand. "You're a smart girl, you know that?"

"But I thought you and Loretta liked Mason."

"Loretta does," Gram said. "I let him come to the house because of her."

"Does he give you the creeps too?"

Gram laughed. "No. Not the creeps....I'm sure

Mr. Mason didn't mean any harm. At times he has a gruff way about him."

"You can say that again," Kathy agreed.

"Let's let it pass for now," Gram said with a wave of her hand. She leaned on the arm of the chair while she twisted to get to her feet. "They're both coming over again tonight. Right now I need a cup of tea to perk me up. While I'm in the kitchen, could you help by setting up the card table?"

Gram limped out of the room while Kathy brought the collapsed table to the middle of the room. She released the legs and set the table upright. Lisa had said it was urgent that her grandma find the deed to the property—and soon. That must be why they were all meeting here again.

Kathy thought about Mason coming to this room. A shiver ran through her. She glanced suspiciously around the room, then went over to the window and ran her finger along the crack below the sill, where that fog had crept in. She whistled the tune from the music box as she started for the stairs to the loft.

If Gram and Loretta were determined to let Mason join them in the seance, then there was only one thing left for her to do. Spy!

CHAPTER
7

Kathy stood at the living room window and watched for Loretta's car in the darkening night. Finally the car pulled up to the curb in front of the cottage, and Lisa jumped out. As Lisa ran up to the porch, Kathy rushed to meet her at the door.

"My grandma said I could come over while they have their meeting," Lisa said. "Isn't that super?"

Kathy grabbed Lisa's hands and pulled her inside. "Can you sleep over too?"

"Not tonight. I've got to watch Digger for a couple of hours tomorrow morning while my grandma goes shopping."

"Where is he?" Kathy asked, looking past Lisa just as Mason climbed out of the car.

"He went to a campfire meeting with another kid from Peace Camp. Just think, now we can talk all we want without him eavesdropping."

The door opened and Loretta came in, followed by Mason. Kathy stepped back to make sure Mason wouldn't brush her as he passed. She felt his stare but did not look up.

"Be good now, girls," Loretta said. "You've got over an hour to visit."

The adults grouped together in the living room and Lisa and Kathy dashed upstairs. "What a perfect place," Lisa said, going directly to the window and looking out over the dark bay. "You can see forever from here."

Both girls were quiet a few moments before Lisa crossed to the bed and sat down. "I heard my grandma talking to my mom on the phone just before we left. My mom told her that my brother—you know, Ruben?" She waited for Kathy's nod. "Well, Ruben thinks that Mason doesn't want Grandma to find that Spanish deed."

Kathy's eyes widened. "Why?"

Lisa folded her arms and shrugged.

Kathy sat down next to her. "Do you think Ruben's right?"

"Maybe. Ruben's a smart guy."

Kathy stood and paced in front of Lisa. "If Mason doesn't want Loretta to find the deed, then he must come to these seances to see if your Grandpa Ramón knows where it is." She stopped in front of Lisa. "If your grandpa knows, maybe Mason—"

"Well, if my grandpa knows," Lisa interrupted, "then he better tell my grandma—and soon."

Kathy went to the window. "Who's at the restaurant tonight?"

"No one. The restaurant isn't open for dinner on Monday."

"Then let's go. This is our chance. We can search Mason's room. Maybe we can find something to show our grandmas."

"I don't know, Kathy. We could get into a lot of trouble."

Kathy grabbed her hooded sweatshirt from the closet. "I know. It isn't nice to snoop. But if Loretta doesn't find that deed, she's in a lot of trouble."

Lisa swung her legs over the bed and stood up. "Okay. Let's go!"

Kathy crept down the stairs with Lisa close behind. Candles flickered in the living room, and Loretta called for Ramón. If Mason had his eyes shut, they would have a chance to sneak past the arch and down the hallway without being seen. If his eyes were open, then....

Before they reached the bottom stair, Kathy pressed Lisa's arm. "After the last step, get down on your hands and knees," she whispered. "When we pass the living room, don't look in. Just keep following me."

Kathy wanted more than anything to know if that eerie fog was hovering around. But she kept her eyes straight ahead while she crept past the archway. Back on her feet, she grasped Lisa's hand and pulled her up. The two headed down the hall for the back door. Lisa stepped hard on Kathy's heel and Kathy winced inwardly, but she didn't make a sound.

Outside, she let out a groan. "Owww, you scraped my foot."

"I'm sorry," Lisa said. "I couldn't see. Too dark." She glanced around the deck. "Now what?"

"Let's get my bike."

Lisa nodded and they ran to the garage and wheeled the bike out to the street.

"How much farther?" Kathy asked after she'd pedaled for what seemed like a hundred miles.

"Three more blocks," Lisa said brightly, sitting back on the seat and enjoying the ride. "Ouch," she complained. "You just sat on my hand."

"Well then, move back," Kathy grumbled. "I have to sit down sometimes."

"Want me to take it from here?" Lisa asked.

"You're on."

When they arrived at La Costa, all was dark. In

back of the house, the girls jumped off the bike and leaned it against the fence behind a row of bushes.

Lisa rushed toward the rear door. "I know where the extra key is, and there's a flashlight in the kitchen." She opened the fuse box at the side of the porch and ran her hand along the metal shelf. She found the key and swiftly opened the door.

Inside, she fumbled through the pantry before she emerged with the flashlight. "If we get caught, I'm dead."

"We're not going to get caught," Kathy said, trying to convince herself as well as Lisa. "But let's hurry." They headed for the steps leading up to the rotunda. This time she followed Lisa, who held the flashlight toward the floor. "Wait," Kathy said, grabbing Lisa's arm. "Is Mason's room locked?"

"If it is, I can get that key too."

They dashed up the steps. Kathy kept her balance by touching the wall. Eerie shadows cast from the streetlight outside made her move even faster. At the top of the stairs, they turned right. Kathy shivered and reached for Lisa's hand. When Lisa turned the knob on Mason's door, it wouldn't budge. Just as Kathy suspected. Locked.

"Stay here," Lisa said. "I'll be back in a second."

Kathy listened intently as Lisa stepped lightly down the stairs and crossed under the rotunda.

Lisa stopped once and flashed a beam of light around where Kathy stood. Then Lisa and the light were gone.

Alone on the balcony, Kathy felt light-headed and dizzy. It must be fear, she told herself. She waited, hardly breathing, glued to the spot for what seemed like a zillion years. When her feet began to feel like bricks, she shifted noiselessly from one foot to the other and pulled her sweatshirt close around her, zipping it up all the way.

Suddenly a voice broke through the silence. "Come on in, matey. Make yourself to home."

Kathy stumbled over to a corner and dropped to the floor, pulling her knees close to her chest and her hood over her head. Someone was in Mason's room! Someone who knew she was out here. She crossed her arms on her knees and buried her face. Lisa, she silently cried, where are you?

CHAPTER
8

Crash! Kathy flinched. What happened? Where was Lisa? She lifted her head. "Oh, no!" she cried, finding herself in a pool of light. She peeped around, then quickly buried her head again.

"What's the matter?" Lisa asked seconds later as she squatted in front of Kathy. "Why are you on the floor?"

Without looking up, Kathy felt for Lisa's jacket and gave it a tug. "That light," she said in a muffled voice. "What is it? There's someone in Mason's room—and what happened downstairs? That noise?"

Lisa pulled Kathy's arm. "Get up! That light is just the moon coming in through the dome. See?"

Kathy peered over her arms. Carefully she inched her way up, keeping her back against the wall. "Okay," she said reluctantly. "But someone's in that room. And what was that crash?"

"I knocked down some cans in the cupboard," Lisa said. "What a mess. I'll clean it up later." She switched off the flashlight and gazed down the hall. Her eyes widened. "You think someone's in there?"

"Don't talk so loud," Kathy said. "I know someone's in there. He told me to come in—and called me matey."

"Matey?" Lisa laughed. "There's no one in there. Come on."

Kathy held back. "I heard him," she insisted.

"What you heard is—just come on," Lisa said impatiently. Trust me."

Kathy followed, glancing around as she moved along the hall. Lisa focused the light on the lock, inserted the key, and turned the knob. Mason's door creaked open.

Lisa stiffened.

When Lisa didn't move, Kathy gave her a nudge. She squinted over Lisa's shoulder at the dimly lit room. Lisa hesitated, then took a deep breath and led the way in. The two girls huddled together. When nothing happened, they moved to the center of the room.

"This is what you heard," Lisa said, shining the light on the wall.

"A clock?"

"It's a talking clock," Lisa said. "I hear it when I'm downstairs sometimes. You know, like a cuckoo clock. Except this bird's a parrot."

Kathy crossed to the wall. "It looks like a model of a sea chest with a pendulum."

Lisa joined her. "Digger told me about it and I've always wanted to see it. Neat, huh?" Lisa reached up and opened the lid. "The parrot must come out of here. It talks on the half hour. Anyway, that's what Digger said."

"It is neat," Kathy said. "But let's look around. We don't have much time. Can I use the flash for a while?"

"Sure. I'm going to search by the window. There's enough light there from the street." Lisa crossed the room to a big wooden desk. She picked up a brass spyglass and peered over at Kathy.

Kathy examined the clock, then moved the beam of light to the right. A parched document the size of half a sheet of notebook paper hung in a wooden frame. Printed at the top was *February 16, 1818.* On a line below in squiggly writing, *100 pieces of eight.* Near the bottom in faded black script was an illegible signature.

The document looked like a receipt of some

kind, a very old receipt. "What are pieces of eight?" Kathy asked, turning to Lisa. But Lisa wasn't there. "Lisa!" Kathy cried.

"What?" said Lisa, her head popping up over the top of the desk.

"Don't just disappear like that," Kathy said irritably.

"I didn't disappear. I'm trying to see what's in these drawers. But they're locked. And I can't find the key."

"Okay, okay. But just stay in plain sight." Kathy moved the light down the wall. Below the framed receipt a shelf jutted out. On the shelf, lying on its side, was a bottle with a ship in it. It must be the ship Digger said he was helping Mason build. She shoved the flashlight under her arm and picked up the bottle. The model ship inside slipped around and she almost dropped it. She carefully set the bottle back in place.

After taking a couple of deep breaths, she aimed the light again. The ship had four tall masts, and neatly printed on both sides were the words *La Frigata Negra.* Spanish? Kathy got down close and studied the bottle. She lightly ran her fingers over the narrow opening. How did they ever get the ship in through that bottleneck?

Directly below the shelf, on a table covered with a cloth, tools lay in an arc like a doctor's instruments. Starting on the left, there was a sharp scalpel, a pair of narrow pointed scissors, razor blades, a chisel, a small saw and blades, two pieces of long wire like bike spokes, needles and thread, epoxy, model paints, six of the smallest paintbrushes she'd ever seen, sandpaper, and colored clay. These must be the tools Mason used to build his model.

Fascinated by the array, Kathy wanted to spend more time there, but she knew she had to keep moving. She would have to ask Digger about the model ship.

Next she scanned the furniture. Not much of that. Just an old metal bed and two large, comfortable-looking leather chairs. Between the chairs stood a tall bookcase filled with musty books. Butted against the bookcase, a cracked glass case with three shelves housed an assortment of guns, knives, and a sword.

Kathy backed away. Why did Mason need all those weapons?

She looked past the desk to the window, where a tripod held another of Mason's telescopes. This one pointed toward the bay. "Find anything important?" she called to Lisa.

Lisa rustled some papers. "Nothing that says anything about La Costa. But there's all kinds of pictures and maps and history pamphlets of the old Carmel Mission." She held one of the pictures up to the window and studied it. "Mason invites Father Eliot to La Costa for dinner sometimes. After they eat, they always come up here."

"Is Eliot the priest over there?"

Lisa made a face. "Yep. That's why Grandma lets Mason board here. She thinks he's a good Catholic."

"Let's ride over there tomorrow and look around."

"Okay," Lisa said. "I'll show you where one of my ancestors is buried. An Indian who helped build that mission."

"A Costanoan?"

Lisa nodded. "How did you know?"

"My grandma told me. Is he buried in an old graveyard? Does he have a tombstone?"

"Yep. And my grandma's really proud of him."

Kathy smiled. "I like old graveyards."

Suddenly Kathy spotted a glint of chrome in the beam of the flashlight. Propped in the corner was a metal stick with a meter and a speaker on the handle. She went over and read the gold letters painted down the side: TREASURE FINDER. She switched off the light and crossed the room to the desk.

Lisa jumped. "Don't do that, Kathy!"

"What?"

"Sneak around like that. I thought you were Mason."

"I'm sure!" Kathy put her hand over her mouth and giggled. "Why? Are you scared of him?"

"No." Lisa shrugged. "But there'll be plenty to be scared of if we get caught snooping around in his room." She looked down at the desk. "I haven't found anything important. Have you?"

"Maybe," Kathy said. "I found a Treasure Finder."

"Oh, that old thing," Lisa said with a wave of her hand. "His metal detector."

"Do you think we could borrow it?"

"Are you crazy? Take something that big out of here? We'd get caught for sure." She took the flashlight from Kathy and rushed over to the corner. "Why would we need this?"

"I read that you can use a Geiger counter to tell if there's a ghost in your house. I could try using this detector at the cottage. See if that fog's a ghost."

Lisa shook her head. "No way! Mason uses that thing all the time. I always see him leaving with it. And Kathy, please stop with the fog stuff. Give it a rest. I'm tired of hearing about it."

"Where does Mason go with this?" Kathy asked, ignoring Lisa's last remark. "What's he looking for?"

Lisa moved closer. "That's what I'm wondering. Detectors are used for finding metal stuff under the ground."

Kathy nodded. "And if the deed to La Costa is buried somewhere in a metal box..."

Lisa grabbed Kathy's hand. "Let's get out of here." She moved toward the door.

There was a loud click. The two girls froze. They waited. The only sound in the room was the tick-tick of the clock's pendulum.

Suddenly a metallic whirring sound came from the wall. Kathy held on tight to Lisa. The whir-ring noise stopped abruptly. Another click sounded and music poured out from the clock. Old-time music—the tune Digger sang and danced to. The same tune that was on Gram's music box.

Lisa let go of Kathy. "It's the hour!" she said, clapping her hands with relief. "The parrot comes out on the half hour and the music plays on the hour."

Kathy let out a huge sigh. "What time is it?" she asked. She used the flashlight to zero in on the clock. "Oh, wow! It's nine. We better get back to the cottage."

The phone started ringing downstairs.

The two of them looked at each other in horror. They ran out the door and Lisa locked it. They flew down the steps past the ringing phone and stopped by the pantry to drop off the flashlight and Mason's key. After stuffing the canned goods back on the shelves, they left by the back door. Lisa lifted and shut the fuse box in one swift move, and before they could count to ten, they were both on the bike, Kathy pedaling furiously as they sped back to the cottage and the safety of the loft.

CHAPTER
9

Back at the cottage, Kathy and Lisa tiptoed across the deck. After carefully opening the back door, they silently made their way down the dark hall, then paused at the arched entrance to the living room. There were no candles burning, and no voices. Kathy turned and felt for Lisa's hand. Where was everyone?

She heard a click and the living room filled with light. "Come in here, girls." Gram's voice rang out with a definite edge.

Kathy moved forward with Lisa close behind. Gram sat rigidly in her armchair, flanked by Loretta and Mason. Gram motioned Lisa and Kathy to come closer.

"Do you know how worried we've been?" Gram began. "Where on earth have you two been?"

When Lisa got within grabbing distance of Loretta, Loretta pulled her close. *"Mi niña querida!* We were about ready to call the sheriff. You know you're not allowed out alone after dark."

"I wasn't alone," Lisa protested. She looked at Kathy. "We were together."

"I want to know where you've been, Kathy," Gram insisted.

Mason hadn't said a word. He just stared. Kathy glared at him. It was his fault that she and Lisa were in trouble. If he didn't act so weird, they wouldn't have been forced to search his room. And right now she wouldn't be forced to tell a lie. Well, not lie exactly. Although she was about to leave something out.

"We're okay," she said. "We just went for a ride." She looked over at the window. "It wasn't that dark when we left. Huh, Lisa?"

Lisa, her eyes shining with fear, nodded.

Kathy watched Mason watching them. His black eyes darted back and forth from her to Lisa.

"My bike has a rear light on it," Kathy continued. "We weren't in any danger."

"Why didn't you ask permission?" Loretta asked. "How far did you go? We called the restaurant." She glanced at her watch and shook her head in disbelief. "It's already time for Dennis to get home. Don't I have enough on my mind? *Esto es el colmo!*"

Kathy gave Lisa a puzzled look. Lisa mouthed, "This is too much!"

"I'm sorry," Lisa said, giving her grandma a squeeze.

Kathy nodded. "I am, too. We didn't want to disturb you. The candles were lit and your financial meeting had already started."

Loretta cleared her throat, glanced at Bev, then dug in her purse for her car keys. She reached for Lisa and pulled her along. Mason put on his hat.

"Kids have to be kept in tow," he said in his gravelly voice as he opened the door for Loretta.

Loretta muttered something in Spanish, then turned and went back into the living room. "I'll pick you up for rehearsal tomorrow, Bev." She leaned over and gave her a hug. "Sleep well."

When they had all gone, Kathy closed and locked the door and stood under the archway. "Guess I'll go to bed now," she said, looking down at her feet.

"Just a minute, young woman," Gram said. "We have to talk. Please fix me a cup of tea, then come in and sit down."

Without looking up, Kathy went to the kitchen to do as she was asked. When she returned to the living room, she sat on the edge of a chair.

Gram began. "What happened tonight was inexcusable, Kathy. Very irresponsible. If it happens again, I'll have to call your parents."

Kathy nibbled on her lower lip and nodded.

Gram stirred her tea. "I know that it must have been thoughtlessness on the part of you kids, but Loretta and I were extremely worried."

Kathy glanced up. "Was Mason worried too?"

"Mason?" Gram frowned. "Why do you ask?"

Kathy shrugged. "Did he wonder where we were?"

"What were you and Lisa up to? What is it you're not telling me?"

The phone rang. Kathy jumped up to answer it.

Lisa's unhappy voice sounded at the other end. "I forgot to tell you there's a rehearsal for the pageant tomorrow. Can you go with me? My grandma's really upset right now, but she'll get over it. We both know she's got more important things to worry about—like the property deed. I just hope she doesn't call my mother."

Kathy held the receiver away from her ear. "It's Lisa," she said to Gram. "She wants to know if I can go to rehearsal tomorrow."

Gram nodded. "Of course. Tell her yes."

"I can go," Kathy said excitedly. "Can I come to your house early? I need you to help me with something."

71

Lisa agreed and Kathy hung up. Gram struggled to her feet. "Get up to bed now, Kathy. It's late. And remember, no more shenanigans."

Kathy reached in the bookcase and pulled out the book about tap dancing. Tonight she'd shuffle around a little upstairs, then give it a try tomorrow at Lisa's. Gram made her way down the dark hall and softly closed her bedroom door. Kathy headed upstairs.

She went straight to the window in the loft to check the weather. No fog tonight! Next she changed into her pajamas and sat on the bed while she flipped through the pages of the tap book. Unable to concentrate on the dance exercises, she kept looking toward the window. There had been something different out there. What?

She clicked off the table lamp and went back to the dark window. Not a breeze stirred. The moonlight made it possible to see far out on the bay to the horizon.

Wait! There was something. Something strange. She scanned the street and the surrounding houses. Nothing. Then a movement caught her eye—down by the garage, where she'd parked her bike. She clutched the curtain and moved out of view in case someone was watching her. There! A dark form. A thief? After her new bike?

The silhouette of a hat showed in the moonlight.

Mason? But he had left with Loretta. She got down on her knees and peered over the sill, but the shadows had swallowed the hat.

She stayed there for a long time waiting. Nothing happened. She rubbed her eyes. Maybe this time it was her imagination.

Wide-awake now, she felt around on top of the chest of drawers for her art pad and colored pencils. Since she couldn't sleep, she would draw. She switched the light back on, crawled under the comforter, and propped up her pillow. She began sketching. First she drew Snuggles, her dog, then Gypsy, her aunt's orange-and-white cat. Her eyes grew heavy. She scrunched down a bit, put her work on top of the covers, and clicked off the lamp. In minutes she was asleep.

A ship with four masts and a black flag pulled into the harbor. An anchor dropped and a swarm of grubby men in ragged pants and vests, with scarves tied around their heads, dropped over the side of the rig and landed with a thud into rowboats. On the shore behind a sand dune, Indian men and women watched, then turned and ran. "Padre—padre," they cried out in warning. "They're here. Run for your lives."

Kathy awoke with a start. For a minute she didn't know where she was. When her eyes adjusted to the darkness, she reached for her tablet, turned on a light, and began to draw furiously. She drew the scene from her dream: the ship, the sailors, and the Indians. She ripped off that page and started a new one. This time her fingers were being directed. By who or what, she didn't know.

She drew a tree. A huge oak. Limbs and leaves in detail. The tree's lower branches curved and turned. On the trunk a carved cross with an arrow at the bottom pointed to the ground.

Kathy stared at the finished picture with disbelief. It was beautiful—better than any tree she'd ever sketched. She compared the pictures. The bay scene was okay, but the tree had been drawn by a real artist. This was not the first time a picture had appeared on her art pad like this. When she was at her aunt's house, she had sketched a beautiful ancestor who had once lived at Wicklow Manor. Someone had directed her fingers that time, too.

She put the pictures aside, and soon her eyes grew heavy. When she awoke, the sun streamed in through the window and she could hear Gram's cane tapping around downstairs in the kitchen.

She jumped out of bed and raced down the steps with both pictures in her hands. "Look, Gram," she said excitedly.

Gram gave her a hug and took the pictures. "My, this is good work," she said. "These look like scenes from Monterey history. Did you copy these from my books?"

Kathy shook her head. "No. I dreamed this one last night," she said, pointing to the ship. "And I don't know where the tree came from."

"Well, wherever it came from, it's excellent, Kathy. I suggest you bring them with us when we go to rehearsal. I know some folks there who will be interested in seeing what you can do."

Kathy wasn't listening to what her grandma said. Her mind was spinning. She knew that her dream was important. And so were these pictures. She studied the drawing of the oak tree. When she drew fast and perfectly like this, she knew someone must be trying to give her a message. But who?

CHAPTER

10

Kathy rode her bike to La Costa. She steered with one hand while she held her rolled artwork in the other. When she arrived at the restaurant, she stopped a minute out front to look at the building. The spooky shadows cast there the night before had given way to the morning sun reflecting brightly off the upstairs windows.

She parked her bike around back and ran up the porch steps to the kitchen. Before she could knock, Lisa called, "Come on in, Kathy."

"How did you know it was me?" Kathy asked.

Lisa flashed a grin. "Guess I'm psychic—like you."

Kathy felt her cheeks burn. "I'm not psychic,"

she said. "At least I don't think I am. I just happen to see things—sometimes." She glanced down at the tube of paper in her hand. Maybe this time, she thought, I have drawn something that happened a long time ago.

"Just joking," Lisa said. "Whatcha got?"

Kathy unrolled her pictures and laid them out on the table.

Lisa, who had been flattening dough in a tortilla press, wiped her hands on a towel and came over to see. "Oh, pretty," she said, picking up the scene with the ship. "Wish I could draw like that."

Kathy handed her the other one. "What about this?"

Lisa raised her eyebrows. "Wow! Beautiful! Looks like a real artist did this one. Did it take you forever?"

Kathy plopped down in a chair. "I can't do this." She pointed to the details of the tree limbs and trunk. "If you get me some paper and a pen or a crayon, I'll show you how I draw."

Lisa searched through a drawer for a tablet and pencil, and Kathy copied the tree. When she finished, Lisa wrinkled her nose. "I see what you mean," she said with a nod. "Yours is okay. But it's not as good." She picked up the original. "So who drew the tree?"

Kathy leaned back and crossed her arms. "I did."

"Yeah, right! What's the joke?"

"No joke," Kathy said. "Someone or something did it. I drew both of these last night when I was alone. The ship in the bay was a dream I had, and the tree, well...I held the pencil, but something else moved my hand." She picked up the paper with the oak tree and shook it. "This has happened to me before. It's some kind of message—or warning."

"Kathy! Is this for real?"

Kathy nodded. "Why would I lie?"

Lisa got up. "Are you hungry? I'm making my special. Loco Tortillas." She went back to the press and closed it down on a ball of dough. When she lifted the lid, she pulled out a circle of dough. She turned and stared at Kathy before she tossed the tortilla on a hot iron griddle. After a minute, she flipped the tortilla over. "This weird stuff of yours scares me."

"I know it does," Kathy said. "Sometimes it weirds me out too." She studied the trunk with the cross and the arrow pointing to the ground. "I think someone was creeping outside Gram's garage last night. It might have been Mason."

Lisa spun around. "Mason? Why?"

Kathy shrugged.

"What time was it?"

"I don't know exactly," Kathy said. "Right after I got done talking to you."

"Couldn't have been him," Lisa said. "He drove home with us. I watched him come into the restaurant. Even if he ran all the way back, he couldn't have made it to your place by then." Carefully lifting the crisped tortilla from the grill, she set it on a cutting board, spread on a generous gob of peanut butter, and reached for the alfalfa sprouts. Next she sprinkled on chopped cucumber and shredded carrots, covered it all with slices of avocado and cheese, and placed it under the broiler.

"Want one?" she asked.

Kathy's mouth watered. "Sure. It smells delicious."

Lisa made another one and joined Kathy at the table. "Okay," Lisa said with her mouth full. She dripped a spoonful of fresh salsa over her tortilla. "I can't believe an invisible someone used your hand to draw that tree. That's impossible."

"I wish you'd believe me," Kathy said. "I think someone's trying to tell me something. Maybe it's one of the spirits from the seance. Maybe your Grandpa Ramón?"

Loretta bustled into the kitchen. "Ramón? Who said Ramón?"

Kathy gulped her food and looked over at Lisa.

"Not Ramón, Grandma," Lisa said quickly. "Kathy said she might have to go home."

"Why?" Loretta asked. "Did you forget something? You're going to rehearsal with us, aren't you?"

"I should call home," Kathy stammered. "I need Gram to bring my sweatshirt when we pick her up."

"Then do it now," Loretta said. "When lunch is over, we'll have to scoot. *Darse prisa!*"

From Loretta's tone, Kathy figured "darsay preesa" must mean "hurry." She made her call to Gram, then followed Lisa out to her room.

"I need to learn how to tap," Kathy announced as soon as Lisa closed her bedroom door.

Lisa twirled around and did a shuffle with her toe. "Great! We'll work on two basic steps, then you can try out for the chorus today."

"Today?" Kathy said, alarmed. "I don't think so."

Lisa looked disappointed. "You don't want to work on steps?"

"No, I do. I mean I don't think I can try out. I only know how to do brushes."

"Good!" Lisa was all business. "Show me!"

Kathy hesitated, then moved over to the bed and held on to the post.

"Not there," Lisa said. "You can't dance on the carpet. Do it on the wood floor."

Kathy tried. First her right foot, then her left. She lost her balance once and supported herself by lightly touching the wall. I do—I do—I do have balance, she told herself.

"Not bad," Lisa said. "But you're so stiff. Relax."
For the next fifteen minutes they worked on toe
slaps and a dig.

"I think you're getting it," Lisa said enthusias-
tically. "Now try it with tap shoes."

Kathy sat down on the edge of the bed to untie
her tennis shoes. Just then Digger swung the door
open and walked in.

Lisa scowled. "Don't just walk into my room.
You're supposed to knock. What do you want?"

"Aunt Loretta sent me. She says if you want to
ride your bikes to the mission you better get them
to the car."

Kathy looked at Lisa. "We're going to the mission?"

Lisa gave a little shake of her head. "Remember?
You wanted to see it?"

"Oh, right," Kathy said, getting the signal. She
smiled weakly at Digger.

Digger stepped in and closed the door behind
him. "Can I go?"

"No," Lisa said. "Why do you want to go with
us? You've been there with Mason."

"Because. I'll get bored at rehearsal."

"How do you know? You've never been to one."

Digger crossed his arms and dropped his chin
to his chest, causing his glasses to slip down his
nose. "Because I just do."

Lisa brushed by him and opened the door. She stood with her hand on the knob. "We want to go to the mission alone—just the two of us. We've got stuff to talk about."

"What about? Last night?"

"Out!" cried Lisa. "And don't touch our bikes." She slammed the door and braced it with her back.

In a second, Digger's face popped up at the window. "Aunt Loretta says to come to the kitchen. Now!"

Kathy couldn't help giggling. When he disappeared, Lisa joined her.

"He just drives me nuts," she said.

Loretta called Lisa from the kitchen door.

Kathy looked out the window at the restaurant. "You don't think Digger knows anything, do you? Does Mason suspect that we were in his room?"

"I hope not. But if Digger knows, he'll let it slip. Then we'll get it out of him."

CHAPTER
11

The Forest Theater was in Carmel, a town about ten minutes south of Monterey. The parking area was packed with cars and buses when Loretta pulled her station wagon in. One bus had a sign lettered across the side that said Children's Traveling Theatre. Another bus announced: Traveling Troupe and Staff Players.

Kathy, Lisa, and Digger jumped out while Loretta helped Bev from the car. Kathy scanned the surrounding trees, then followed everyone up the slope to the stage. "There really is a forest here," she said, amazed.

"A small forest," Loretta replied. "At one time this area had acres of forest. Now most of the land is filled with homes." She sniffed the pine-scented air. "This outdoor theater is almost a century old."

"Century. That's one hundred years," said Digger, catching up.

"And the stage is called an amphitheater," Loretta continued, smiling down at him.

"Amphitheater!" Digger stated. "Seats rising around a central arena. Arena! A stage—"

"Make him stop!" Lisa yelled, holding her hands over her ears. "Why does he have to do that?"

Loretta patted Lisa on the shoulder. "That's how he learns. Just let him go. Mr. Mason is teaching him a lot."

Digger darted ahead and merged with the crowd gathered around the foot of the stage. Kathy spotted a pretty woman with long red hair standing center stage and holding a mike. "Welcome everyone," the woman said. The microphone let out a high-pitched screech. She turned and motioned frantically to one of the people by the amplifier system.

When the noise stopped, the woman cleared her throat and continued. "All of the directors here today..." She searched the crowd and pointed to Gram. Then she found a man with long hair and a silver earring. Finally she motioned to a younger woman wearing a floppy hat. The red-haired woman introduced Gram as the dance director, the man with the earring as the drama director, and the woman with the hat as the music director.

"All of our directors," she started again, "join me in thanking you for donating your time and energy for this Hispanic Heritage Pageant. On this stage, we will do a reenactment of Monterey history, beginning with the year 1770, when the Spanish explorer Gaspar de Portolá and Father Junípero Serra first set foot on this land. The final scene will be 1846, when California became part of the United States."

Kathy looked around at all the smiling faces and felt a lump in her throat as she remembered Loretta's lost deed. If that important record wasn't found soon, Loretta would lose the last plot of land left from her Spanish heritage.

The woman moved to the edge of the stage. "We would like you to know," she continued, "that we plan to use all of you here in some capacity for this production."

Kathy looked around again. Lots of people here, she thought. All ages. Were they all going to audition to dance?

When the woman with the mike stressed that there would only be two more rehearsals before Friday's performance, Kathy poked Lisa. "Today is Tuesday. I can't learn to dance by Friday."

Lisa nodded thoughtfully. "That is soon, huh?"

"How can everyone learn their parts by then?"

Gram hobbled up alongside Kathy. "Practice for the pageant has been going on all month. The directors have been working with their departments independently."

Gram held Kathy's rolled-up artwork. "I'd like you to go up on the stage where they're painting the scenery and tell Mark, the fellow in the red T-shirt, that you're my granddaughter." She unrolled the art. "He's in charge of the scenery and sets. I have a feeling he'll be very interested in these."

"He will? Why?"

Gram handed her the picture. "Because he needs lots of help getting the scenery painted." Just then some people came up and started talking to Gram.

Kathy moved closer to Lisa. "Do you already know your dance?"

"Yep. I do. Your grandma has been working hard with our tap class. We're doing a dance called La Cachucha." She raised her hands and clicked her fingers. "We're going to use real castanets, but we haven't got them yet."

"Then how can I be part of the chorus?"

"Easy," Lisa said. "Just go up there and do those steps we worked on." She glanced around. "You won't be alone. I'll bet most of these people are here to audition."

"To dance?"

"To march—to dance—to sing. You know, background stuff."

Kathy felt a knot form in her stomach. "I don't know, Lisa."

"You said you wanted to surprise your grandma."

"I do," Kathy said. "But this is all different than I expected."

From up on the stage Gram motioned for Kathy to join her. Kathy left Lisa behind and climbed the steps. Gram took her arm and directed her toward Mark. She introduced Kathy and showed Mark the pictures. Kathy's cheeks felt hot. How come Gram had pushed her back here to the scenery? Did she suspect that Kathy planned to try out? Was Gram embarrassed by her own granddaughter's awkwardness? Kathy backed away so she couldn't hear what they were saying.

Digger sat at Mark's feet mixing paints. The right lens of his glasses was spattered. "You going to help?" Digger asked, blotting a big board with globs of orange.

"I hope so," Mark said, turning to face Kathy. "This sketch you did is great! We need you. Do you suppose you could copy this drawing on that panel over there?" He pointed to a set where three teenagers were working. "This scene is just what we've been looking for. Fifteen minutes of the show revolves around the privateer Bouchard's attack on Monterey in 1818. And here you've got it! Panel Three is where it will go. It needs to be big, though. There's a ladder here you can use."

So. That's what her drawing was all about. Her dream and the picture of the ship were about a privateer called Bouchard. Mark said Bouchard had attacked Monterey. She studied her picture. These guys going over the side of the ship must be headed for shore. They looked like pirates.

Tonight she'd look through Gram's books and find out who Bouchard really was. Mark had called him a privateer. Did privateer mean pirate?

She stepped back to view the other artwork. The first completed panel had the date lettered at the top in black: June 3, 1770. Below, printed in royal blue: Explorer Gaspar de Portolá meets Father Serra. The explorer was planting the flag of Spain on the shore, while Father Serra hung a bell from the branch of a huge oak tree.

On the next panel was the first mission in Carmel, San Carlos Borromeo, made of poles and mud. Near a Spanish bell, a small group of Indians made pottery. Kathy forgot about dancing and the chorus as she watched Monterey history being created with paint. She gave Mark an enthusiastic nod. He handed her an oversized shirt to cover her clothes and got her started.

She sketched the ship and the sailors and the Indians. Then she began stroking in bright colors. Taped music blared as people paraded across the stage behind her, and she could hear Gram's voice calling out directions. She turned once, spotted Lisa at the far side of the stage in her red-and-gold costume. They exchanged smiles and Kathy returned to her work.

"Nice pirate flag. Good work," Mark said later, startling her as she put on a finishing touch of black. "But you don't have to rush, Kathy. You've got two more days to finish."

Kathy stepped down from the ladder. It didn't feel like she had rushed. She looked around. Most of the other scenery painters had left. Digger sat out front next to Gram. Lisa stepped from backstage dressed in her jeans and sweatshirt.

"Sorry you didn't try out," Lisa said. "But your scenery is great!"

"Not bad," Kathy said while she took off the shirt. "I have to admit it's good." She twirled around to look at her grandma, but Gram was busy opening a bag of popcorn for Digger. Kathy felt a twinge of guilt. Maybe by next year, if she learned a few steps really well, she could make the chorus.

"Come on," Lisa said. "Let's get our bikes and go over to the mission. It's neat over there."

They stopped by Gram and Digger. "Where's Loretta?" Kathy asked.

Gram looked up. "She went back to La Costa. She'll be here at four to pick us up."

"Did she leave our bikes?" both girls said at once. They giggled.

Gram nodded. "They're propped over there by that boulder. Be careful now. And don't be late."

Digger sulked as they took off. "I could have ridden him," Kathy said. "He's not that heavy."

Lisa shook her head. "He'll listen to everything we say."

Kathy had to agree as they jumped on their bikes and took off down the hill. They drove along Ocean Avenue with its quaint shops and art galleries, made a left turn on Junipero Street, and pedaled on past cottages and shingle-covered houses until they reached the Carmel Mission Basilica.

"I can't believe this," Kathy said after they parked their bikes and went through the back entrance to the courtyard. "This place looks a lot different than that scene the girls are painting at the theater. This church is huge. Look at the big dome with the bell tower." Kathy pointed. "Wow! Eight bells."

She ran to the bell tower stairway. "What a switch," she called to Lisa. "The first mission in Monterey only had one bell. And it hung from a tree."

She crossed to the flower beds, leaned over, and sniffed. "Look, Lisa," Kathy said. Three humming-birds whirred past her head and hovered over the flowers.

She walked over to the pond in the center of the courtyard and watched three goldfish.

"Where's the cemetery?" Kathy asked.

Lisa jumped up. "We have to go to the front courtyard. Come on, I'll show you."

They passed through a short hall and came out in front of the chapel. An enormous star-shaped window stood over the arched door.

"Over here," Lisa called. She stood by an open wrought-iron gate that led through a stucco wall. "Come and see my ancestor's grave." She walked down the path, stopped, bent down, and straightened a bouquet of flowers in a glass. "My grandma puts fresh flowers here every Sunday."

Kathy joined her and stood at the foot of the grave. She read the words chiseled in the headstone:

IN MEMORY OF AMBROSE
WHO DIED
APRIL 8, 1880
AGE 108 YEARS
BAPTIZED BY REV. FRA JUNIPERO SERRA
THE FIRST MISSIONARY OF CALIFORNIA

Kathy looked at Lisa, her eyes wide. "He lived to be that old? Wow!"

"Awesome, huh?" Lisa said. "I wish I could have known him." A sad look filled her eyes, and she kneeled down.

"Look," Kathy said. "Someone carved a feather at the bottom of the stone. What kind is it?"

"Grandma says it's a seagull feather. I guess he liked birds. I've always felt sorry for Ambrose. He was blinded in some accident when he was young. He lived here until he died."

Above the courtyard wall, Kathy could see the fog moving in from the sea. She pulled her sweatshirt closer around her, then stopped short. To the left of the headstone, fog was also forming—taking shape. Kathy blinked. The fog moved slowly, circling the stone. The finger Kathy had seen at the cottage lengthened to an arm that wavered back and forth.

This time the finger pointed at Lisa!

CHAPTER
12

"Look!" Kathy whispered, moving closer to Lisa. "Do you see it?"

Lisa looked up. "See what?"

Kathy motioned with her head. "Over there."

Lisa peered at the headstone. "What?"

Kathy watched as the fog rose sharply then spun over the top of the chapel.

Lisa leaped to her feet and squinted at the tiled roof. "What are you looking at?"

"Nothing now. It disappeared. It was the fog. That ghostly one."

"Oh, Kathy!" Lisa complained. "Stop it!"

"Why?" Kathy said. "It was here. And it was hanging around Ambrose's headstone."

Lisa glared at Kathy. "Don't bring your spooky stories around Ambrose's grave. That's disrespectful."

Kathy's eyes narrowed. "Maybe it is, but that spooky fog pointed at you."

"At me! Come on. You're just trying to scare me."

"I am not," Kathy replied quickly.

"Why don't you stop looking for stuff that isn't real?" Lisa asked.

"I don't look for stuff. This eerie stuff finds me. And it is real." Kathy turned and started for the gate. "Come on. Let's go."

The two girls raced through the hall to the back courtyard.

"Look," Lisa said. "There's Father Eliot."

The priest emerged from a narrow arched doorway. Directly behind him walked Mason.

Kathy reached for Lisa's arm and pulled her back into the dimly lit hall. "Yikes! It's Mason," she said in a low voice.

Lisa shrugged. "So what?"

"Do you think he followed us?"

"Why would he want to do that?"

Kathy frowned. "Maybe he wants to ask us why we snooped in his room."

"I don't think so. If he suspected anything, he'd have told my grandma—and Digger would have said something by now."

They watched from the shadows as the two men crossed the courtyard. Halfway across, Mason stopped, pulled out a big handkerchief, and blew his nose. He spotted the girls in the corridor and stared.

Kathy felt a chill grab her bones. When the men were out of sight, she clutched Lisa. "Let's get out of here."

Later, Loretta picked everyone up at the Forest Theater, then drove back to Monterey and dropped Kathy and Gram off at the cottage. "Same time tomorrow?" she asked.

Gram nodded and Kathy waved at Lisa and Digger as the car pulled away from the curb. Then she ran ahead to the porch and held the door open for Gram.

After dinner, Gram looked out the front window at the fog rolling in from the bay. She lit a fire in the fireplace. Within seconds, the fire crackled.

"Did you and Lisa enjoy your trip to the mission?" Gram asked, adjusting the fireplace screen.

"Yep," Kathy said, plopping down on the sofa. "It was awesome." She told Gram in detail all about the bell tower, the courtyard with the pond, and the beautiful flowers.

Gram nodded. "I knew you would like the colors. Flowers bloom there all year long." She pulled the drapes shut, then settled herself in a chair across from Kathy. "Did Lisa take you to Ambrose's grave?"

Kathy nodded. "He was really old when he died, huh?" She remembered the fog blanketing Ambrose's headstone. "And guess what?" she said, then stopped herself. Should she tell Gram?

"Yes, Kathy? What?"

Kathy bit her lower lip. "Mr. Mason was there too," she said quickly.

Gram leaned forward. "Did he speak to you?"

"No. He was talking to the priest."

"Father Eliot?"

Kathy nodded. "Do you know him?"

"I've met him," Gram said, her voice trailing away.

Kathy blurted out, "Gram, Mason's creepy."

Gram sat quietly. "Mason is a writer," she finally said. "A historian doing research on the Costanoans. I agree that he has a sinister quality. He stares a lot. But I think that's because he's lost in his work. Very eccentric."

She gazed at the flames shooting up from the log. "He says he picked out La Costa as a place to stay because of its history. Plus the fact that Loretta's a descendant of the Costanoans." Gram looked thoughtful. "If you think about it, what he says makes sense."

Kathy nodded, but she wasn't convinced. She knew Gram and Loretta thought that she imagined things. Oh well, she'd tried. But grown-ups had their own way of thinking.

Besides, after what happened today at the mission, the way the ghostly finger had pointed at Lisa, Kathy had more important things to worry about. She sure hoped Lisa wasn't in any danger.

Later, up in the loft, Kathy unlocked the window. She gazed out at the whirling fog before she got into bed and snuggled under the quilt. She was so tired that soon the world went dim around her. Then she saw something strange in her mind. A face with dark, empty eyes.

She opened her eyes and the face vanished. The cottage was dark. As a gentle breeze rustled the leaves of a tree outside, Kathy closed her eyes, turned over, and fell into a deep sleep.

A lurch of her bed brought her awake. The moon shone through the bedroom window. The night had cleared. The fog must have drifted back out to sea. She heard a tiny sound. What could it be? The click of a door closing? Wide-awake now, she stared into the darkness. She listened. Silence. But she felt a presence in the room. She knew she wasn't alone!

Suddenly a thump came from the closet. She pulled the blanket up. When she found the courage, she peeked over the edge of the blanket and glanced toward the corner. A chilly breeze parted the drapes on the window just as a muffled sound came from the closet.

A damp, salty smell filled the room. Kathy's eyes watered and her nose began to run. She inched her way to a sitting position, clutching the quilt to her chin. She reached for a tissue on the table next to the bed, then pressed back against the pillow and sat motionless. The moon cast a pale shimmering light, and the floor creaked.

From the corner of her eye, Kathy could see the fog stream out from beneath the closet door. It rose to the ceiling, formed into an uneven ball, then drifted down to the side of her bed, where it floated side to side in a ghostly dance. Kathy watched without moving. Finally she called out in a small voice, "Hello?"

The instant she spoke, the fog spread out and up, taking human shape. A man? Two black holes opened in the head, like eyes. Kathy sat perfectly still, watching.

The phantom drifted back and forth from the window to the bed. Then with a swoosh, it passed through her closed bedroom door. Kathy let out a rush of air. She had been holding her breath without knowing it.

She slipped out from under the covers, opened the door, and tiptoed to the top of the steps. She listened. No sound downstairs. She walked back to her bed and sat on the edge. Why hadn't she just asked the fog what it wanted?

Loretta hadn't been able to see the phantom. Lisa couldn't see it. And Gram thought it was just some old mist that settled in. Since Kathy was the only one who could see it, maybe the phantom was trying to tell her something. But what? It didn't matter if the phantom carried a good message or a threat, she had to find out what it was!

Suddenly she heard a ting-a-ling downstairs. A bell? Kathy cocked her head. She made her way carefully down the dark stairs and stood under the archway. On the bookcase a candle burned next to the crystal bell.

As Kathy watched, the candle rose and floated across to the fireplace mantel, where it settled beside the antique music box. Then, without the lid being lifted, the music box began to play slowly. Kathy backed up against the wall.

There it was! The phantom's dark eyes focused on her from the corner of the ceiling. Kathy felt like turning and running as fast as she could back up to her bed. But she didn't. She took a deep breath and waited to find out whatever the phantom needed to tell her.

The fog floated down the wall in time to the music. She watched as it floated across the mantel and pointed to the music box. The music stopped, but the finger continued to point.

Kathy crossed to the fireplace. She stepped up on the stone hearth and the fog moved aside. With trembling fingers, she examined the music box. The candle gave off just enough light for her to see the words engraved on the bottom: Rio. The Secret to the Future Is Found in the Past.

She read it twice, then looked over at the fog. It flew up to the ceiling, circled, then dropped to the hearth. It rested a moment near Kathy's feet. Then it flew up the chimney. The candle flame went out. Kathy clutched the music box to her chest, turned, and ran up to her room.

CHAPTER
13

"Did you have a restless night?" Gram asked Kathy the next morning.

Kathy sipped her orange juice. "Kind of. Why?"

"I thought I heard you in the living room around midnight."

Kathy munched on an oatmeal muffin, picked out the raisins, and grabbed an apple.

"I heard music," Gram continued. She opened her wallet and took out two one-dollar bills. "Here. In case you need spending money."

Kathy shoved the money in her fanny pack and fastened it around her waist.

"Did you open the lid on the music box last night?" Gram asked.

"Yep," Kathy said, avoiding Gram's eyes. "Then I took it up to the loft. I played it until I went back to sleep."

Gram studied her face for a moment. "Why couldn't you sleep? Is something bothering you?"

Kathy shook her head. "I went to sleep. Then a noise woke me up. And that fog came in my room and—"

"The mists again," Gram interrupted, shaking her head. "These old homes have all kinds of crannies for the moisture to seep through. Slits under the windows, keyholes, chimneys."

"This one came in through my window," Kathy said quickly. "I left it open. And it was the same one that floated around down here the first night I came."

Gram smiled. "The same one?" She lifted an eyebrow. "You sound as if this mist has a personality."

"It does!" Kathy insisted. "And it's not just a creeping mist. It's a fog that swirls around and points."

Gram looked thoughtful. "What did it point at last night?"

Kathy had almost decided to tell Gram everything, starting with the fog on Ambrose's tombstone. How at first she thought the phantom fog might be trouble, but now she wasn't sure. Should she show Gram what she'd found on the bottom of the music box? And tell her how the phantom fog had led Kathy to that message?

But before she could make a decision, a car horn out in front honked.

"There's Loretta," Gram said, reaching for her cane. "Time to go to rehearsal."

In the car on the way to Carmel, Kathy was dying to tell Lisa about what had happened. But Digger sat between them. He wore a T-shirt with a whole population of prehistoric beasts on it.

Lisa asked him to switch places with her, even tried to bribe him with seventy-five cents, but he wouldn't budge.

Rats, Kathy thought. She'd have to wait to tell Lisa later.

The Forest Theater was buzzing with activity when they arrived. She left Lisa and the others behind and went directly up on the stage. She got one of the oversized shirts, a paintbrush, and two small cans of paint. Climbing the ladder to work on her panel, she felt someone watching her. She turned around and Mason was in the theater, sitting about six rows up.

What was he doing here? Quickly turning back to her scenery, she tried to pretend that he wasn't there. But it didn't work. A vision of Mason's eyes kept flashing at her. Her goal for the day was to finish the faces of the pirates scrambling over the side of the ship. But how could she work with him watching? She hunched up her shoulders and shuddered. The old creep!

Kathy thought a moment and smiled to herself. If Mason was going to sit out there all day, she'd give him something to stare at. She looked at one of the faceless characters she had drawn yesterday, the one hanging over the side of the ship clutching onto a rope. She sketched in Mason's face. Bushy eyebrows—black eyes. Then she painted in the beard and streaked a mean curved line for the mouth.

She was about to turn around and face Mason when she remembered something. The pirate's right hand. Using the tip of the brush, she gave a firm flick and painted out half of the little finger.

Now Mason really had something to stare at! She turned with a defiant look. But he was gone.

"Great pirate's face," Mark said, strolling up. "You really have a talent for expressions." He held his chin while he studied Kathy's work. "Need more paint?"

Kathy pointed to the brown and yellow cans. "I'll paint the ship a rusty orange and the masts yellow. Okay?"

"Just keep doing what you're doing," Mark said, moving on to the next panel, where a teenage boy worked at painting Father Serra at the Carmel Mission. "You sure don't need any help from me."

Lisa stopped by next. She wiggled the foot of the ladder. Kathy didn't see her. She used both hands to hang on and almost dropped a paint can. "Don't do that!" she cried.

"Eeee," Lisa said, stepping back. "Grouchy! I just wanted to get your attention."

Kathy settled down. "I thought you were Mason. He's hanging around here someplace."

Lisa looked out past the stage to the seating area. "Relax. He doesn't suspect anything. If he did, I'd have heard."

Kathy set her paint cans on the tool tray of the ladder and climbed down. "Okay. Here I am. What?"

Lisa frowned. "I have to watch Digger when we're through rehearsing. He wants to go to Point Lobos and look for fossils. I have to take him."

Kathy felt a pang of disappointment. She wanted to be alone with Lisa so she could tell her about last night. "Where's Point Lobos?"

"It's a state park. It's not that far, but we can't ride our bikes on Highway 1 because of the traffic. My grandma's going to drive us there. Then we can ride our bikes into the park. Grandma'll come back and pick us up at five." Lisa made a face. "If you don't want to go—"

105

"I do," Kathy said, using a cloth to wipe the paint from her hands. "Digger doesn't bother me that much." She looked over her shoulder then back at Lisa. "I've got something really important to tell you."

Lisa moved closer. "What?"

"Not now," Kathy whispered.

"Why?"

Kathy looked around suspiciously. "Because Mason might be listening."

"Who cares?"

Kathy started up the ladder. "I do. You'll just have to wait."

When Kathy finished her project for the day, Lisa was still rehearsing. Her dance group had goofed up the first time around, and now Gram insisted that the junior tappers wait and run through their number again. Kathy sat down in the first row next to Gram and watched them. She had seen most of this yesterday and soon she gave a bored yawn.

"You can ride your bike over to the library and read," Gram suggested. "It's just a few blocks from here. Right behind the park on Ocean Avenue."

Kathy didn't answer right away. Gram reached over and gave Kathy's knee a little nudge.

Kathy smiled. "I heard you, Gram. I was just thinking. Do they have a history section?"

Gram nodded. "I'll bet they have hundreds of books on the history of California and the Monterey Peninsula."

Kathy jumped up. "Good! Can Loretta pick me up there?"

Gram checked her watch. "How about three? Lisa can run in and get you."

Kathy started for her bike. She stopped and turned around. Mason was nowhere in sight. "Where's Digger?" she called back to Gram.

"He's with Mark," Gram said, pointing to the stage. "He's painting near the bottom of one of the sets."

Digger was on his knees making bold brown strokes with a heavy brush. Kathy could see that he was really into his work. She shrugged and took off at a run.

CHAPTER

14

The library stood right behind the park where Gram said it would be. After locking her bike to the stand, Kathy went in. A couple of kids sat in front of computers rattling the keys. Except for them, the room was practically empty.

The librarian at the desk, a dark-haired woman with bright eyes, helped Kathy fill out a form for a temporary library card.

"I'm looking for books about Monterey history—mostly pirates," Kathy requested. The woman led her to an area filled with history books.

Kathy picked out four books and went to a table and spread them out. The first one she looked at, *Pacific Privateers,* had a huge sailing ship on the cover. Flipping through the pages, she decided privateers was just a polite name for pirates.

But wait! She flicked back through the book. She gasped. That colored reprint of a painting was almost identical to the picture she had drawn that night in her bed. The one she was working on at the Forest Theater.

Eager to share her find, she let out her breath and looked around the room. No one here would care—or believe her. When Lisa came to pick her up, Kathy would show the picture to her.

Kathy studied it right side up then upside down. This ship had the same four masts as hers, but there were more men scurrying over the side. She peered at the side of the ship: *La Fr.g..a N..ra.*

The ship's name was partially covered by the dangling legs of the men. Could this ship be *La Frigata Negra*? The same name as Mason's model ship in a bottle?

Kathy gasped again. That pirate with the red kerchief tied around his head and the knife jammed in his belt—his hand clinging to the rope had only half a little finger. Kathy moaned and rolled her eyes toward the ceiling. On the panel at the theater, she had drawn Mason's face on that same pirate. She slammed the book shut.

The librarian raised an eyebrow and glanced pointedly at Kathy. Kathy smiled self-consciously and carefully opened the book again. Starting at the bottom of the page below the picture, she read fast.

On a November morning in 1818, cannon fire boomed from a ship in the bay of Monterey, fired by Hippolyte de Bouchard, a Frenchman commanding an Argentinian privateer ship. He sent a note to the governor of Monterey demanding surrender of the city and all of the King of Spain's belongings.

The Spanish soldiers at the Presidio fired back, then retreated. Bouchard's men went roaring into town, and after stealing everything they could, they set fire to all the buildings before they sailed away with their loot.

Kathy turned the page to a chart that showed how the wounded privateers were compensated for their injuries.

Loss of right arm—600 pieces of eight (one dollar)
Loss of finger—100 pieces of eight.

Wow! That's what had been written on the framed receipt in Mason's room—100 pieces of eight. A pirate's loss of a finger had to be worth—she figured in her head—one-sixth of a dollar. That would be...not even seventeen cents. Unreal!

She closed her eyes, concentrated, and tried to visualize the document. That receipt on the wall had been signed, but the signature was illegible.

Someone plopped down in the chair next to her. Kathy opened her eyes. "Lisa!"

Lisa picked up one of the books. "Pirates, huh?"

"Yeah," Kathy said. "I'm going to check this book out. You've got to see this picture."

"Not now," Lisa said. "We have to go. Grandma's double-parked out front." She groaned. "With Digger."

Lisa returned three books to the shelf while Kathy checked out one at the desk. Then the two of them rushed outside to where Loretta and Digger waited in the station wagon.

Lisa helped Kathy get her bike on the car rack. "Where's Gram?" Kathy asked.

Loretta rolled down the window. "Bev had to stay for a meeting with the other directors." She motioned to the bike rack. "Be sure that bike is on there good and tight, girls."

Lisa gave a tug and nodded. Then she opened the car door.

Digger, next to the far window in the back seat, moved over and made room for Lisa in the middle.

"You can have the front seat now," Lisa said.

He took off his glasses and stuffed them in his pocket. "I don't want it."

Lisa frowned and got in. Kathy hesitated with her hand on the door. She spotted Mason on a bench in the park. At least from behind it looked like him. She climbed in and poked Lisa. "He's over there," she whispered.

"So?" Digger said. "He always goes to parks. He likes to read there."

Lisa scowled at him. "Who? How do you know who Kathy is talking about?"

"You guys always whisper about Mason." He leaned forward. "Huh, Aunt Loretta?"

Loretta wove the car through the busy street. "Don't tease Dennis, girls," she said distractedly.

Ten minutes later they were at the ranger station at Point Lobos State Park. "The greatest meeting of land and water in the world," Kathy read from a brochure handed to her at the entrance gate.

Loretta took an air gauge from the glove compartment and used it on all of their bike tires before she let them go off on their own. "Wear your glasses," she warned Digger. "And if thick fog moves in," she called after them as they pedaled away, "get back to this gate as fast as you can and wait. I will be here at quarter to five."

112

Digger zoomed past Kathy and Lisa.

"Wait for us," Kathy hollered.

"I'm going to Whaler's Cove," Digger shouted back, standing up on his pedals.

"Digger!" Lisa commanded. "Get back here!"

Digger did a wheelie, made a quick U-turn, and almost ran into her. "Why? I know where I'm going."

"Maybe you do," Lisa said. "But we don't. Just stay with us." She stopped and referred to the map the ranger had given her. "How do you know where you're going, anyway?"

"Mason showed me. He's got a big map." Digger circled around the two girls. "Just follow me."

Lisa looked over at Kathy and Kathy nodded. "Okay. But don't go too fast."

He took off like a bullet and Lisa and Kathy frantically worked their pedals in an effort to keep up. He raced down the road and made a quick right at the sign pointing to Whaler's Cove.

Suddenly they were surrounded by meadows filled with yellow daisies and blue and apricot-colored wildflowers. The road angled downward and immediately Kathy was sailing along the side of the cove with a sea mist brushing her face.

Digger stopped abruptly, got off his bike, and went to the edge of the cliff. He knelt down. "Ship-wrecks and sunken treasure are at the bottom," he said, peering into the dark waters. "And see those cavities in the rocks? That's where the pirates hid their treasures."

Kathy looked out over the inlet of water. Of course. Ships could have dropped anchor here and no one would have seen them. "Did Mason tell you about the treasure?"

Digger nodded. "He says there's a ton of gold down there." Digger looked over at Kathy, his eyes shining with excitement. "He's got a metal detector. And if I help him find the treasure, we're going to build a clipper ship 360 feet long and 226 feet tall. Just like the one we're building in the bottle. Then we're going to sail away to the Komodo Island and look for Komodo dragons." He reached for a stick and swirled the pointed end in the water. A large black bird with a long neck floated close to the shore and ignored them as it rode a wave.

"Yeah. Right," Lisa said, moving her bike closer. "Dragons. I'm sure!"

"Just wait." Digger turned to face her. "You'll see when we bring one back. They're 12 feet long and weigh 300 pounds. They have skinny bodies and powerful legs and they smile like a crocodile." He turned back to Kathy. "They're really lizards and they're the closest living relative of the dinosaur."

"Do they bite?" Kathy asked.

Digger shook his head. "The one I catch won't.

Mason says the dragon will like me." He gazed out over the bay to the horizon. "And I'll call my dragon D.M."

"D.M?" Lisa asked. "What kind of a name is that?"

"A good one. Those are Mason's initials."

Lisa laughed.

"Digger," Kathy said carefully.

Digger pulled in the stick and placed it on a rock. "What?"

"What's Mason's first name?"

"Why? Who wants to know?"

"I do," Kathy said.

"He doesn't like people to know his business."

Lisa let out a sarcastic laugh. "Well, too bad! His name is Drago—Drago Mason."

CHAPTER
15

Digger jumped on his bike and headed back to Whaler's Cabin, an old structure made into a museum.

After he left, Kathy paced around on the road. "I've got all this stuff to tell you and a picture to show you." She threw her arms in the air. "Darn! I left the book in the car."

Lisa squinted. "What kind of a picture? And why did you want to know Mason's name?"

Kathy looked thoughtfully at the water as it lapped against the rocks. "There's this picture in the book that's almost identical to the one I drew the other night. The one I'm painting for the pageant." She stopped to think. "And I needed to know Mason's name because…I'm really not sure. Something I read—in his room."

"What? Where?" Lisa asked. "Did I see it?"

"I don't know. It's in a frame on his wall," Kathy said. "Some kind of an old document like a receipt. It had a signature at the bottom."

"So? He has lots of old stuff in his room."

"I know that," Kathy said. "But this—" She began pacing again. "So what do you think? About the drawing?"

"Weird."

"Weird is right! Something's going on." Kathy's voice lowered. "That phantom fog was in my bedroom last night. Then he went downstairs, moved a lit candle—played Gram's music box— danced around the ceiling—"

"Whoa," Lisa cried, holding up her hands. "Don't tell me about it!" She shuddered. "You're calling that creepy fog a he? And now he dances?"

Kathy backed off. "Okay. I won't tell you everything I saw. I know you don't want to hear it, but just listen to the message I found on the bottom of the music box Loretta gave Gram."

"Do I have to?"

Kathy ignored her and stated the words she had memorized: "Rio. The secret to the future is often found in the past."

Lisa's eyes widened. "So?"

"Secret—future—past," Kathy repeated firmly. "What do you think that means?"

"I don't know," Lisa said. "What makes you think it's a message? Sounds like an old Spanish saying to me. That's probably why my grandma bought it. She's always hunting around antique stores for stuff like that."

"It's a message all right," Kathy said. "The fog led me to it."

"Oh, right, that fog again." She shook her head. "I don't think so, Kathy. I think you've lost it."

Kathy dug her toe in the dirt, then looked up. "Well, I don't," she said confidently. "After last night I trust this phantom. And it's hard to do—because I've always hated fog." Her eyes lit up. "But when I see it again I'm going to ask questions."

"You want to see it again?"

"Yes," Kathy said. "And if this phantom wants us to follow his instructions, we will."

"We?"

Kathy looked into Lisa's eyes. "Do you want to save La Costa?"

Lisa nodded reluctantly. "You know I do. But following a fog isn't going to help."

"It might."

Lisa leaned back on her bike seat and studied Kathy's face. "You're serious, huh?"

"I need help with this, Lisa," Kathy said.

"Okay, okay," Lisa said. "But I don't like it."

A shout came from the cabin. "Over here, you guys."

Lisa looked over at Digger, then back at Kathy. "I'll help. But I don't want to be around when you think you see that fog floating." She gave a push on her pedal. "Come on. I can't lose Digger!"

When the girls rode up, they found Digger in back of Whaler's Cabin, crouching with his hands on his knees. "I can't believe this," he said, inspecting the outdoor display. "A real fin whale skeleton. Look at that skull bone. And wow! A spinal column." He stood up alongside the bleached bones. "I think it's a Basilosaurus isis. An early ancestor of the whale. Or it could be a Mesonychidae. A meat-eating wolflike mammal that whales evolved from."

"Really?" Kathy said. "If they ate meat, they had to live on land. Right?"

"They did," Digger said. "Fifty million years ago. Their feet were eight inches long and they had three teeny-tiny toes." He ran over to the other side of the whale's spinal column and picked up a small rock. "I bet this fossil is one of its toes." He brushed off the dirt, adjusted his glasses, and examined it.

"How come you know so much about fossils?" Kathy asked. "Does Mason tell you all about them too?"

Digger brought out his magnifying glass and studied the rock. "Nope. He doesn't know anything about stuff like this. My mom and dad are paleontologists. They study prehistoric fossils and plants."

Kathy looked over at Lisa, who was busy examining a huge rusty pot on a tripod. "No wonder he's so smart," Kathy said.

Lisa nodded. "Get him to show you a picture of his dinosaur egg. His parents brought it back to him from China."

Before Kathy could ask him, Digger had jumped on his bike and pedaled off, coasting down the hill toward the end of the road, which was filled with parked cars. Lisa and Kathy grabbed their bikes and managed to stay close behind.

To the left, the land rose sharply. Digger spotted the flat rock stairs, dropped his bike, and darted up the steep steps.

"Digger," Lisa yelled. "Don't go up there alone. Wait for us."

But Digger just kept going. Higher and higher. The girls ran up after him. By the time they got to the landing, Digger had veered off to the left and was racing up another set of stairs made from railroad ties. He headed toward the cliff.

"I'm going to strangle him," Lisa said, panting. "Where's he going?"

"I don't know," Kathy said. She looked over her shoulder to the bottom of the steep rise, where their bikes lay sprawled.

Lisa muttered something in Spanish. Then she turned to Kathy. "I'll go get the brat."

Kathy nodded. "I'll watch our bikes." She looked over the other side of the landing, toward the sea and the rocks and the waves crashing loudly below. "And if you don't strangle him, Lisa, I will."

She waited on the landing for what seemed like forever until all the cars parked below had gone. Each time a wave smashed against the rocky shore below, great swirls of saltwater and foam shot up and covered her with a cold spray.

She pulled her sweatshirt hood over her face. Then, folding her arms tightly across her chest, she hugged herself.

Where was Lisa? And Digger? The fog was rolling in. She watched as it slunk over the rocks like a gray cat, then rose in shifting clouds.

She made a lunge for the steps and ran up. But the fog trailed after her. By the time she reached the top of the stairs, the fog was so thick she could barely read the sign—it said Whaler's Knoll, with an arrow pointing up to a place called Cypress Grove. Kathy hesitated before climbing higher. There were no stairs now, just a path crisscrossed with gnarled tree roots. The trail above her had already been socked in by the fog. No way would she be able to see.

"Lisa! Digger!" she yelled. Nothing. Her words were swallowed up by the sound of the thunderous waves. She tried again. "Lisa!" She waited a moment, then started back down the thick wood steps while she could still see the way. Reaching out to the side, she grabbed a wire cable attached to metal posts. Holding on tight to the handrail, she made her way to the landing.

She cupped her hands around her mouth and made one more call. Even if they heard her and answered, she thought, she'd never be able to hear them above the crashing waves.

She tried to see the bikes, but the cove was blanketed with fog. She had better get down there. She held on to the wire and started down the flat stone steps. Slippery! She was three steps down when her foot went out from beneath her. She grabbed for the ice plant, a thick low-growing ground cover on the side of the hill, but her fingers slid from their slippery stems.

Regaining her balance, she wiped her hands on her jeans and remembered that she'd seen poison oak on her way up. That was the last thing she needed!

When her feet finally touched packed-down sand, she heaved a sigh of relief. But that feeling didn't last long. In the parking area she could only find one bike. Hers! The other two were gone.

Kathy stood in the mist and looked around. She felt so alone. Had Digger and Lisa taken another path down, grabbed their bikes, and left her behind? Digger might do that. But Lisa never would. She and Kathy were friends.

The density of the fog made it impossible for her to see much, but she could hear the *splash, splash* of the water as it slapped against the cove's craggy shoreline. The sharp smell of seaweed almost made her gag.

From above came squawks from seagulls, and she smiled uncertainly. She wasn't alone after all. Even if she couldn't see them, there were birds and animals out there.

She started walking her bike. Maybe the others were waiting for her at Whaler's Cabin. She squinted but the cabin wasn't visible. A shuffling noise behind her made her stop. Some animal making its way across the road through the fog? *Shuffle, shuffle.* Closer now. It sounded like footsteps. She jumped on her bike and started pedaling toward the cabin as fast as she could.

CHAPTER
16

Kathy took a gulp of the misty air and forged ahead. The hill that had been such fun coasting down now became a chore to get up. She could only see about two feet ahead. She stopped short when the big cypress tree next to Whaler's Cabin suddenly loomed before her.

Okay, okay, she told herself, stepping back. It's only a tree. But with veils of moss hanging from the branches, and the way the branches dipped to touch the ground, the tree looked like a sea monster.

She circled the cabin, searching for the other two bikes. When she couldn't find them, she propped her bike against a boulder, then rushed up the two stone steps to the door. Darn! Padlocked. The woman at the entrance gate had warned them that the museum closed early today.

She peered in a window next to the door. No one was inside. Now what? She had really expected Lisa and Digger to be here. Maybe something awful had happened to them. Maybe they didn't get their bikes at all. They could still be up on the trails, lost in the fog, stumbling around and tripping over those gnarled roots.

Maybe someone took their bikes. She glanced anxiously toward the road. Someone who shuffled.

She sat down on the step to think. Waiting here wasn't going to do her any good. She'd better try to find her way up to the park entrance, wait for Loretta there, and tell her what happened.

Back on her bike, she pedaled up the road. A howling somewhere off in the distance made her feet move faster. Sea lions? Wolves? The brochure said the Spanish word *Lobos* meant wolves.

She rode on until she reached a sign, Official Vehicles Only. This was the wrong road. She'd made a wrong turn. But that was okay. There would be rangers down there. She rushed on until she hit a Dead End sign—no official cars or trucks in sight.

There was only one thing to do now. Turn back the way she had come. Back to a locked cabin. By now her fingers were wet and cold as she gripped the handlebars. She rode faster, determined to find her way back.

Invisible birds and animals continued their eerie concert. Once she thought she heard the shuffling noise behind her. She didn't look back. By the time she reached the cabin, she was shivering.

After circling the cabin again, she dropped her bike out back, raced around the building, and shoved on windows until she found one that would budge. Spotting an old rusty wagon wheel a few feet away, she rolled it to the wall, propped it up, and stood on it. With one giant heave, the window opened wide enough for her to slip through. Then it slammed shut.

She looked around inside the dimly lit room. On the walls were fishing nets, seashells, pictures, and an old ship bell. In the center of the room were tables and books. Straight ahead, a doorway opened into a smaller room. A light switch on the wall to her left caught her attention, and she gave it a flick. The ceiling fixture flashed on and off. She tried again. This time it didn't even flicker.

She crossed to the front window and looked out. Nothing but fog, and the barely visible road. Suddenly a rumble shook the glass, and a ranger truck rolled by. Kathy pounded on the window. "Hey!" she shouted. "I'm in here!"

The truck didn't stop. She ran back to the window where she had climbed in. She pushed and pulled and shoved, but now it wouldn't open. "Come on," she insisted, grunting and heaving. But it was jammed shut. She knew the truck had to turn around, because the road circled back. If she didn't catch their attention on their way back, and if the fog didn't lift, she might be stuck here all night.

Too late! Another rumble and the truck passed the cabin. Kathy raced to the front window, pounded, then stood helplessly as the truck disappeared. She slumped down on the floor and heaved a huge sigh.

The dense fog left droplets of water on the windowpanes that streamed down the glass like tears. Kathy felt like crying. But what good would that do?

She got up and wandered around the room. She would just have to wait for Loretta. Loretta would surely find her.

Before long she got interested in the history of Point Lobos. She read old newspaper clippings and looked at pictures on the walls. Thirty-one Hollywood movies had been filmed at this cove. Old ones. Some of them scary. She shuddered.

She looked at framed pictures of shore whalers in 1862, men who harpooned whales less than ten miles offshore. The men sat in their small boats with their harpoons and lances while they towed the captured animals to the beach, where the whales were then flensed—stripped of their blubber. Once the flensing was complete, the whalers tossed tons of blubber into big pots, built fires, and melted it down for oil. Those pictures made Kathy sad.

She moved on. In the smaller room, she stopped at a black-and-white drawing of the early Costanoans. A dozen people with caked mud on their bodies gathered acorns.

The next picture showed the Indians much later, dressed in European-style clothes, working with the padres at the mission. To the right, three men squatted around a bowl, using slender spoons to fill long feather quills with yellow sand. Kathy peered at the caption beneath the picture.

Gold! They were filling the quills with gold. The Indians had found golden pebbles near the mission. They filled the feathers and stored them away in a safe place in case pirates invaded Monterey.

Pirates!

A shadow crossed the front window. Kathy froze. The brim of a black hat and a round nose pressed up against the glass.

Oh no! Kathy silently cried. Mason!

"The lass is in here," he bellowed.

Loretta's station wagon screeched up next to the cabin and Lisa jumped out in a flash. "Kathy!" she said, pounding on the window. "Let me in."

Kathy motioned to the side window. "That one," she cried.

While the two girls worked on opposite sides of the glass to open the window, Digger got out of the car. Loretta immediately ordered him back in. Finally the window sprung up and Kathy climbed out. Loretta pulled her close in a bear hug. "*Mi niña querida,*" she cried.

"Jeez, Kathy," Lisa said, wringing her hands. "I'm so sorry." She sent a dark look in Digger's direction. "He took off his glasses, left the path up there, and slid down that steep hill. I didn't want to leave you—but I didn't know what else to do."

She winced and showed Kathy her palms. "Look at these scratches. I had to slide down after him and follow him over a hundred roads before he led me to the entrance."

Mason held the car door open while the girls got into the back seat. Loretta kept Digger up front between her and Mason.

"How come Mason came with your grandma?" Kathy whispered to Lisa.

"He didn't," Lisa said. "He was already here. Grandma picked him up at the gate."

Mason turned around. He must have heard Kathy mention his name. She slouched down on the seat. Had Mason made that shuffling noise behind her on the road?

For the next few minutes, they drove along in silence. They passed artichoke fields on their right and beaches on their left. When they passed the Carmel River the next street sign read Rio Road.

"Lisa!" Kathy whispered. "Rio Road!"

Lisa glanced out the window then back at Kathy. "So?"

"Rio—remember? The music box."

"Rio's Spanish for river," Lisa said.

Mason turned again. "Rio Road runs alongside the Carmel River," he said. "And the river runs through the mission." He waited. When neither of the girls responded, he faced front again.

Kathy became silent. This Rio Road might be important. She'd tell Lisa what she thought later when Mason wasn't around to listen.

They picked Gram up at the Forest Theater. Digger stayed in the front seat and Mason moved to the back. Kathy scrunched closer to Lisa and gripped her hand.

For the next ten minutes, Loretta told Gram what had happened at Point Lobos. Lisa leaned forward, and when Loretta stopped to take a breath, Lisa filled in with her side of the story.

Gram turned to Kathy. "Are you all right, Kathy? You're not saying much."

Mason stared at her.

"I'm okay," she said, leaning back against the seat, away from him. "I just got cold."

Gram studied her face. "What would you have done if the park had closed and you weren't able to find Loretta?"

"I had the two dollars you gave me and I saw a bus stop on the highway."

Mason gave a wheezy laugh. "A smart one, she is. No need to worry about her." He twisted to face Kathy. "Then you'd have left the cabin, would you?"

"Of course she would have," Lisa said impatiently. "You don't think she'd have stayed in there all night, do you?"

Gram nodded. "The three of us will discuss it when we get home."

"Three?" Kathy asked, surprised.

"Yes," Gram said, putting her arm around Digger's shoulder. "Digger's staying with us this evening. Aren't you, honey?"

Digger gazed up at Gram and smiled sweetly.

"And you'd better mind Bev," Loretta said in a threatening tone. "If I hear any more reports about your behavior, you'll be grounded."

Lisa nudged Kathy. "Good luck," she said. "We're going to Santa Cruz to meet my mom and my brother for dinner. It's about an hour up the coast." She nodded toward her grandma. "They're going to try to figure out how to remove that cloud from the deed—whatever that means." She leaned back and gave a huge sigh. "Too bad we have to pick up the brat later."

CHAPTER
17

At dinner, Kathy watched Digger shove the last bite of French toast in his mouth and wash it down with a gulp of milk. "We never have breakfast stuff for dinner," he said, using a spoon to scoop up the last drop of maple syrup on his plate. "I like it!"

Gram looked at Kathy and smiled. "I do, too. You did a fine job of cooking, Kathy." Her eyes flicked back to Digger. "French toast has been a favorite supper dish in the Wicklow family for generations."

Kathy nodded. "My dad fixes it for dinner on Saturday nights. He uses thick slices of sourdough—the kind of bread the California gold miners used." She took a bite. "This is my favorite. French raisin bread, sprinkled with cinnamon."

When they were through eating, Gram stood and reached for her cane. "I'm going in to watch the news," she said. "Our local TV station is giving the pageant a spot tonight." Her eyes shone. "They're going to interview the music director."

Digger surprised Kathy by immediately helping her clear up the dishes. He wiped down the counters and rinsed out the frying pan before filling it with hot water and detergent.

"Why did you zoom off and leave us today?" Kathy asked as she stacked the plates in the dishwasher. "I think it was stupid for you to run around up there on those cliffs. What if you or Lisa had fallen?"

Gram came back to the kitchen to get her cup of tea. "Kathy's right, Dennis. I know you're in enough trouble with your aunt Loretta, but your thoughtless actions left Kathy alone in a strange place. Not only were the surroundings at Point Lobos strange to her, but the whole area was covered by fog. Any one of you could have been hurt."

Digger looked down at the floor.

"I don't want to lecture you," Gram continued. "But please think about what I've said." She gave him a pat on his back. "You know what's right and wrong. You're a good kid."

After Gram left, Kathy persisted. "So why did you act like that? You made Lisa so mad."

"I don't care," he said stormily, picking up a scrubber and working on the pan. "I didn't want to come to La Costa. My parents made me. If Lisa doesn't like me, that's tough!"

Kathy knew all about parents sending you places you didn't want to go. But so far, her parents' choices had turned out to be adventures for her.

"You'll be going back home soon," she said. "School starts in another week. And haven't you had any fun since you've been here?"

"Sure I have," he said. "Lots of fun with Mason."

"Right. You guys are building a ship in a bottle, huh? That must be fun." Her mind flashed back to two nights ago in Mason's room, when she'd almost dropped it. "I've always wondered how to do that. Tell me, Digger. Please?"

"I don't know if Mason wants me to."

"Why? It's no secret," Kathy insisted. "Mason didn't invent how to do it. But if you really don't want to tell me, I guess I could go back to the library and find a book that will explain it." She shut the dishwasher door and turned it on. "But we haven't got anything else to do. Why don't you just tell me how?"

"Well," Digger said halfheartedly. "If you really want to know..." He added quickly, "Don't tell Lisa. Promise?"

Kathy used her right hand to cross her heart. "Promise!"

"It's simple! Just build the ship outside the bottle then collapse it."

"Collapse it? Then what?"

Digger sighed. "Guess I'll have to start at the beginning. I need paper and a pencil." He pulled out a chair from the table, sat down, folded his arms, and waited.

Kathy went to the loft then returned with her art pad and pencils. "Do you use charcoal?" she asked. "I've got plenty."

"Nope. Just need a pencil." Digger adjusted the paper. "First you have to have all the right stuff," he said, printing a list of the tools Kathy had seen for herself on Mason's table. "And then you have to have patience."

Kathy watched as he drew a rough sketch of a ship.

"This is supposed to be a schooner," he said, cocking his head and holding the paper out. He looked at Kathy, who had settled down in the chair next to him. "Mason carved the hull to scale, then he gave me sandpaper and I did the smoothing down. Some people make models with a kit and a plastic bottle." He shook his head in disdain. "Mason says that any mariner worth his salt would never do that. He says that if a real seaman saw

136

one of those fake models he'd have a severe bout of the shudders."

"Looks pretty good," Kathy commented as Digger slanted the pencil to fill in the sides. "How about the masts?"

"Be patient," he scolded. "I'll draw them. But first you have to rig it with slivers of wood and thread. All the masts are made on tiny hinges that collapse." He quickly drew the rigging with long controlling threads dangling down. "Then you make the sails out of white cotton and fold them back so that once the ship is inside the bottle you can haul the masts up."

He drew a flat cross under the ship. "This is the wooden rigging base. The ship sits on it—then it's eased on through." He sketched a bottle exactly like the one in Mason's room. He pointed to the neck. "See, the ship goes right in here." He made arrows darting across the page, through the neck to the inside of the bottle. "Then you pull the base out and leave the threads hanging through the neck. When Mason pulls on them, the masts pop up."

Kathy studied Digger's sketch. "What happens to the threads? Are they left dangling?"

"Nope. Mason holds the threads together with a rubber band and carefully places them inside the bottle." He set the pencil down. "That's it!"

Kathy smiled. "Fantastic! Can I see the picture?"

Digger handed her the paper, then stood and stretched. "We're going to build a real schooner next. Mason's going to start it as soon as he finds the lost treasure. Then he's going to sail away and take me with him."

"To the Komodo Island," Kathy said, remembering Digger's story about the dragons. "But first you have to help him find the treasure. Right?"

Digger nodded. "Yeah. Mason told me to keep my eyes and ears open."

"Do you think your parents will let you go that far away? And what kind of treasure is it?"

"Lost treasure," Digger said.

"What kind of lost treasure?"

"You know. Sunken or buried."

Kathy opened the fridge. "Want some grape juice?"

Digger nodded. Kathy filled a glass for him and put four Fig Newtons on a plate and set it on the counter. "You don't really think your parents will let you go the Komodo Island, do you?"

Digger took a bite of his cookie. "I don't see why not. They go all kinds of places around the world on their digs and never take me. If they don't let me go with Mason," he said firmly, "that wouldn't be fair."

Kathy thought she saw the starting of tears in

the corners of his eyes. "That's their job, though," she said, trying to make him feel better. "Parents can't take their kids with them to work."

Gram called to them from the living room. "Come and see. Here's Amanda."

A fire was crackling in the fireplace as Kathy and Digger went in. On the TV screen, the music director wore the same floppy hat pinned with a flower. She talked about the meaning of Hispanic Heritage Month and the historical pageant of music and dancing.

"How come you're not dancing in the pageant?" Digger asked Kathy. "I saw you practicing in Lisa's room."

Gram looked up, surprised. "Lisa's teaching you to tap?"

Kathy felt her cheeks burn. "Just messing around."

"If you're serious about learning to dance—"

"Maybe next year," Kathy said quickly. "This time I'm okay with painting the scenery."

Gram nodded and went back to watching the TV screen.

Kathy sighed. Well, she'd done it again. Disappointed Gram.

There was a knock at the door and Digger ran to open it. "Aunt Loretta's here."

But it wasn't Loretta. Mason stood waiting on

the other side of the door. "Your aunt sent me," he stated gruffly.

Digger opened the door and Mason lumbered in. His eyes scanned the room and rested on the music box. Had he heard Kathy tell Lisa about Rio?

"Hello Mason," Gram said. "Is Loretta back from Santa Cruz?"

Mason stood in the hallway. "She called to say she'd be later than planned and that I was to pick up the lad."

"Are you going directly back to the restaurant?"

Mason nodded. "The boy will stay in my room. I'll settle him down on the sofa."

"You don't have a car," Gram said. "That's a long walk."

"Not that far," Digger said, looking up at Mason with admiration. "We walk a lot farther than that sometimes, huh?"

Mason stared at Kathy, then his eyes shifted to Gram. "Well, now, what do you say? Can we be leaving?"

Gram hesitated. "All right," she said. "If that's what Loretta wants. But please have her call me when she gets home. Tell her it's important."

CHAPTER
18

Kathy watched from the doorway until Mason and Digger disappeared around the corner. When she went back into the living room, Gram, still in her chair, poured lotion into the palm of her hand from a small amber bottle. Bending forward, she carefully applied the lotion to her leg.

"How's your knee?" Kathy asked, peering at the pink skin where the Ace bandage had been. "Does it still hurt?"

"It's starting to feel better," Gram said. "Your aunt Sharon sent this." She checked the label on the bottle. "Arnica Lotion. Sharon said this would take the soreness and stiffness away. I've been using it for two days now and I believe she's right!"

Kathy leaned over and sniffed the bottle. She took hold of Gram's hand and read the label. "This is made from Montana flowers." She looked puzzled. "How can flowers help?"

Gram finished rewrapping the bandage and rolled down her pant leg. "For centuries all healing agents were made from herbs and flowers. Your aunt studies them and uses them. When she sends me a remedy, I always try it. I trust her." Gram straightened her leg out, then bent it back. "See there. No pain."

Kathy jumped up and clapped her hands. "Great! Let's go for a little walk."

Gram smiled. "I'm not ready for that yet. But if the knee continues to heal at this rate, I'll soon be able to toss this old cane."

Kathy crossed to the bookcase and ran a finger across the spines of two books on the middle shelf.

Gram picked up the newspaper from the end table and checked the TV section. "There's a good musical on tonight," she said brightly. *"Annie.* Have you seen it?"

Kathy shook her head. "I need to read tonight, Gram. I brought a book from the library that has pictures of pirates."

"Books come first," Gram said. "I'm happy you're a reader. I don't have any books about pirates, but there's a book on the top shelf with a good chapter on the early Carmel Mission. The book has gold embossed printing on a tan cover."

Kathy pulled the book. "Can I take it to the loft?"

"Sure. Go ahead," Gram said. "I think you'll enjoy reading about the mission's early days."

Gram's right, Kathy thought later as she settled back on her pillow and flipped through the chapter describing the mission. But soon she set Gram's book aside and picked up the library book. The mission would have to wait. First she wanted to read more about pirates.

She found the place where she'd left off at the library and reread how the pirates who lost body parts got a bigger share of the booty. On the next page was a picture of Hippolyte de Bouchard, dreaded Pacific privateer, holding his gloves in one hand, his hat in the other, and dressed in a flashy blue uniform with brass buttons and gold fringe on the shoulders. He had mean black eyes.

Soon she was deeply absorbed in the account of how the buccaneer had dropped anchor from *La Frigata Negra*, the black ship, late one night out in Monterey Bay. Her eyes widened. He had sent his first mate, Mondragon—Mondragon?— to shore with a note to the governor threatening to reduce the city to cinders. Then he had sent a number of his men in several small boats, and they landed on the beach.

Kathy turned back the pages to the picture of the boat with the men scrambling over the side. Mondragon must be that guy with the kerchief tied around his head, the knife in his belt, and the missing little finger.

She shivered. Drago Mason. Could Drago be short for Mondragon? Could Bouchard's first mate have been some ancestor of Mason's? Gram would be interested in this. Kathy jumped from the bed. Clutching the book, she ran to the top of the stairs. In three leaps she made it to the bottom and darted into the living room. On the TV the song "Tomorrow" blared while Gram dozed in her recliner.

Kathy stopped and cautiously made her way over. Gram looked so peaceful with her head back and her lips slightly parted. Kathy leaned over just as Gram let out a light snore. No need to wake her.

Kathy opened the book again and studied the picture and the name Mondragon. The longer she thought about it, the weirder it all seemed. She slowly made her way back up the stairs to her room.

After setting the book about Bouchard on the chest of drawers, she picked up the book about the mission. Back in bed, she propped up her pillow and pulled up the quilt, then settled down to read again.

Wow! This book told about Bouchard, too. How the padres, not wanting to risk losing the church valuables when the pirates landed, loaded their prized possessions onto the back of an Indian called Ambrose, who was sent inland to bury it all.

Kathy looked up from the book in disbelief. Ambrose! Lisa and Loretta's ancestor?

Kathy read fast. Ambrose had done as he was told. When he returned to the mission, the city was in flames. The pirates had already robbed stores, destroyed orchards, and burned buildings. Ambrose ran to help put out the fires, got trapped by falling timber, and burned his eyes. Blinded by the smoke and fire, he somehow made his way back to the mission.

When Ambrose reached the priests, he told them where he had buried the church valuables. By the river. Rio Carmel. He had carved a large cross on an oak tree above the site and an arrow at the base of the tree. Beneath the arrow lay the treasure.

But the treasure was never found. Ambrose couldn't see to lead the padres there, and though they searched up and down the river and the surrounding area, they never found the tree.

Kathy jumped up and crossed to the window. "I can't believe this," she said out loud. "The phantom must be Ambrose! He wants me to find the church treasure."

She opened the window to let his foggy presence in, but the night was clear. Disappointed, she crossed to the dresser and rummaged through the top drawer. The picture of the tree, the one she had drawn two nights ago, was gone. Where? She had definitely put it in here. She searched each drawer, but the picture was gone.

A sudden chill raced down her back. She ran over and jumped under the covers, flicked off the light, and buried her head. Tomorrow she'd tell Lisa everything, no matter what. Lisa had to believe her now. Kathy stretched her legs out and finally relaxed. As she fell asleep, she thought she heard the ting-a-ling of the crystal bell.

CHAPTER
19

The next morning Kathy opened her eyes to bright sunlight streaming in the loft window. She stretched and yawned and turned on her side. As she lazily stared over at the wall, her eyelids flickered and closed.

Her nose itched. She wiggled it, sniffed, sneezed twice, and sat up. She ran her finger back and forth under her nose. Then she opened her eyes, scooted around to her knees, and stared at her pillow. There at the side lay a long, silvery feather. A seagull feather.

Without moving her head, she glanced from side to side. "Hello," she called out softly. "Anyone there?"

When there was no reply, she inched her way over to the edge of the bed and cautiously placed her feet on the carpeted floor. On tiptoes, she crossed to the closet, carefully opened the door, and held it wide. If the phantom was in there, she'd give him plenty of room to come out.

She waited with her hand on the doorknob but nothing happened. She peered in. Except for her clothes, a few loose hangers, and her suitcase on the floor, the closet was empty.

She ran back to the bed, jumped on top of the quilt, and sat down. Gingerly, she picked up the feather. She gazed at it steadily, waiting for something—or someone.

Nothing in the room moved. All was silent. The phantom must have visited her during the night. Vaguely she recalled the sound of the crystal bell.

Too bad she had slept so soundly. Thoughtfully, she twirled the quill. The feather wasn't filled with gold, the way the picture on the wall at Whaler's Cabin had described, but someone had carved a feather just this size at the bottom of Ambrose's tombstone. This must be a sign.

Did the phantom want her to follow him and find the tree with the cross and the arrow?

The church treasure was important, but Kathy had to admit that she felt a pang of disappointment. She'd hoped to be able to tell Lisa that the phantom fog would lead them to Loretta's missing deed.

But what if they followed the phantom Ambrose and found the church treasure? That should make Loretta and Lisa happy, since it was their ancestor who had buried it. And lost it.

She quickly dressed in white shorts and a red shirt, ran a comb through her hair, slid the feather behind her ear, and gathered up the books. She rushed from the loft to show Gram what she'd found. Gram would have to believe her now. But as she started down the steps, a hum of voices came from the living room.

Halfway down, she crouched and peered down into the living room. Gram, the other two directors from the pageant, and the announcer, the red-haired woman, were there. Suddenly Amanda, the music director, must have said something funny because Gram trilled a high laugh. The others instantly joined her.

Gram spotted Kathy on the stairwell and waved. "Come in here, Kathy," she called. "Meet my friends."

All eyes were on Kathy as she walked down the steps. She could feel the gray-and-white feather trailing over her ear.

After Gram made the introductions, Amanda pointed at Kathy's head. "I like your feather," she said with enthusiasm. "It shines just like the one on top of that music box over there." She pointed at the fireplace mantel.

Kathy reached for the feather and examined it.

"Do you collect them?" the long-haired man asked.

Kathy shook her head. "No." Then with a flustered look, she nodded. "Yes!" She added in a shaky voice, "sometimes."

Gram rescued her. "The pageant performance is tomorrow," she said pleasantly to Kathy. "There's a lot to do today and I'll be here and there and everywhere. After you eat breakfast, can you ride your bike to La Costa and go to rehearsal with Loretta?"

Kathy nodded again and crossed to the hall.

"I'll meet you at the theater later then," Gram called.

Kathy sank into a chair in the kitchen, relieved to be alone. What a shock. Another feather—and right on top of the music box. The phantom must have left it last night. Well, there would be no time to talk to Gram today. Kathy would have to convince Lisa about the treasure.

On her ride to La Costa, Kathy had the books tied to the back of her seat with a bungee cord. She had wrapped the feathers in plastic and placed them between the pages.

When she reached La Costa, she went directly around back, took the books, and went to Lisa's room. She knocked on the window and went inside.

Lisa met her at the door in her pajamas. "Hi," she said brightly. "Look at the sun." She began rummaging through her top drawer and brought out shorts and a top, trying to match the colors Kathy had on. "Let's go to the beach before rehearsal."

"Lisa," Kathy said in a somber voice. "We can't."

Lisa looked disappointed. "Why? Do you have to go someplace?"

"We both do."

"Oh no! Not the phantom again."

Kathy nodded. "I need to go back to the mission graveyard. I don't know why yet, but you promised to help."

Lisa pulled on her shorts and shirt and sat down on the edge of the bed. Kathy joined her. She opened Gram's book and turned to the chapter about the early days at the mission. After removing the plastic holding the feathers, she let Lisa read about Ambrose.

While Lisa read, Kathy waited. When Lisa finished, she set the book down beside her. "How sad. I didn't know about the church treasure. I'll bet my grandma does, though. That's why she puts flowers on his grave every Sunday, huh?"

"Probably," Kathy said. She carefully took the feathers out of the bag and placed them side by side on top of the book.

"Seagull feathers," Lisa stated, picking one up. "Pretty. Where did you get them? Did you walk on the beach this morning?"

"Nope."

"Okay. What's wrong?" Lisa said. "Tell me."

Kathy hesitated, took a deep breath, then told Lisa who she thought the phantom was, why he had helped her draw the picture of the tree with the arrow, and why he left the feathers at the cottage.

Lisa jumped up. "Are you crazy? That old fog can't be Ambrose. He's been dead forever."

"I wish the phantom would let me see him again," Kathy said, more to herself than to Lisa. "I want to ask him some questions. But when I woke up this morning, he was gone. I wanted to tell Gram, but she's too busy today. Maybe Loretta should know."

"My grandma?" Lisa shook her head. "I don't think so. She's upset enough over the lost deed. When we were with my mom and brother last night, she couldn't even eat her dinner. Ruben told her he suspected Mason of being a con man."

"Why?"

"Ruben doesn't trust him. Thinks he might be

after the deed to La Costa." Lisa looked at Kathy. "Maybe you've been right about Mason."

Kathy's heart began pounding in her throat. "Yes!" she said. "I knew it. He's not only creepy, he's a crook." She started pacing. "But why? What can he do with the deed if he finds it?"

"Ruben says he can destroy the deed, then bid on La Costa at a public auction after the county forecloses on the property."

"What did Loretta say?"

"She told Ruben he has an overactive imagination. And that Mason would never think of doing anything to jeopardize the future of La Costa."

Kathy nodded. "Well, I think Ruben's right. Don't you? That's why Mason's been coming to the seances. He's trying to find out if your Grandpa Ramón knows where that Spanish deed is. Maybe he plans to get to it first and burn it or something."

"Well, if my grandpa knows where that deed is, he better start saying. Grandma's only got ten days to find it. If the county takes La Costa, she'll never get over it."

Kathy agreed. "We have to tell someone about Mason." She studied the feathers in her hand. "And about these—and the phantom."

Lisa thought a moment. "If we're going to the mission, how about Father Eliot? Maybe he'll believe you."

153

Kathy nodded, wrapped the feathers, and put them back in the book. "He might. Let's go and see."

They rushed out to get their bikes. Kathy hesitated and looked over at the restaurant. "Aren't you going to tell Loretta where we're going?"

"She's not here," Lisa said. "She's at your gram's studio practicing with the Time Tappers for the pageant."

"Loretta's going to dance?"

"Her group is. Grandma says she'll join them if she can pull herself together."

Kathy looked up at the second-floor window. "Is Mason up there?"

"Nope," Lisa said. "He took Digger camping last night. They went over by the river."

Kathy's stomach lurched. "The river! Why there?"

Lisa shrugged as she wheeled her bike away from the fence.

"Let's hurry," Kathy said.

"It's a long ride to the mission."

"I know," Kathy said. "We can make it."

For an instant, their eyes met. Lisa took a deep breath then started out. "Follow me," she called.

CHAPTER
20

When Kathy and Lisa finally reached the Carmel Mission, they climbed off their bikes and sprawled on the grass, exhausted from the long ride.

"Look," Kathy said a few minutes later, pointing to the tops of the trees. "Fog!"

Lisa lifted her head. "You think that's Ambrose?" she asked warily.

"No. He's not that big. Let's go find Father Eliot."

"You'll have to go," Lisa said dramatically, resting her wrist across her brow. "I can't move."

Kathy felt just as tired as Lisa. "Five minutes!" she said crossly. "Then we'll both go in."

"Water," Lisa begged. "I need a drink."

Kathy got to her feet. "I do too. Isn't there a fountain inside?"

Lisa nodded.

"If I can find a paper cup," Kathy said, "I'll bring one back." She made her way into the front courtyard and searched the grounds. No Father Eliot in sight. She walked past the sanctuary to the back courtyard.

Her eyes rested on the gate to the cemetery. She changed her course and soon found herself at Ambrose's grave, shivering at the foot of the mound as the fog blotted out the sun.

Suddenly a feather floated down in front of her face. Kathy took a step back. The feather landed softly on the grave, directly beneath the carved feather on the headstone. She looked up. Nothing above her. No birds. Not even a tree.

She squatted and picked up the feather. Another sea gull feather. Silvery, just like the others. She stroked the feather thoughtfully. Turning abruptly, she rushed to show Lisa.

"Look," Kathy said. "Another one. It fell from the sky and landed on Ambrose's grave."

Lisa sat up. "It's a seagull feather all right. And it's shiny," she said. "Just like the other two. Where are they?"

Kathy frowned. "I left them in your room." She

twirled the feather. "The phantom will be here soon. I just know it." Her eyes scanned the area. "When he shows up, we'll follow him."

Lisa yawned and stretched. "I don't think I can."

Kathy gasped. "There he is!" She lifted her bike and jumped on.

"Where? Show me."

Kathy started pedaling while she pointed toward the road. The phantom moved swiftly above her, flying over the moving cars. When Kathy got too far behind, the fog stopped and hovered in place, just long enough for her to catch up.

"Kathy," Lisa called from behind as she pedaled furiously. "Wait!"

Kathy glanced over her shoulder but kept on going. She couldn't stop now. She might lose sight of Ambrose. At the first intersection she slowed and looked up at the sign. Rio Road. On she went, past the shopping center, past houses and condos, until she was stopped by a yellow metal railing with a sign that said Dead End.

On the other side of the railing was a freshly plowed field dotted with new artichoke plants. The field bordered a golf course on the far side. From where Kathy stood, straddling her bike, she could see a golfer swing, then move on out of sight.

Where was the phantom?

To her left, beyond the field in a grove of trees,

a gauzy film of light floated in and out of the branches. Ambrose? She glanced back over her shoulder as Lisa pulled up beside her.

"What's your problem, Kathy?" she said irritably. "Thanks a lot for waiting!"

"Sorry," Kathy said. "I had to keep going. He moved too fast for me to stop."

Lisa glanced around suspiciously. "Where is it?"

"In those trees, I think. See that faint light?"

Lisa squinted and nodded uncertainly. "I think so. I see something. Is that Ambrose? I thought you said he's a fog."

"He is," Kathy said. "Or he was. Looks like he's brightening." She propped her bike against the railing. "Come on. We'll have to walk. This ground's too soft to ride on."

Lisa grabbed Kathy's arm and pointed the other way, toward the river. "What are they doing here?"

Kathy blinked. Mason! With a shovel. And Digger carrying the metal detector! She took Lisa's hand. "Hurry before they see us."

Too late! Digger cut in front of Mason and waved frantically above his head. Mason strode swiftly to keep up with him and in seconds they were both headed their way.

"No!" Kathy cried, racing toward the trees. "Hurry. Let's hide."

"Yeah, or I'll have to take care of Digger."

Kathy shook her head. "No. It's more than that." She ran as fast as she could, her tennis shoes sinking into the newly turned earth. After every step, she had to pull with all of her might to get her foot out. Lisa, right beside her, hauled her own feet, ignoring Digger's calls for them to wait.

When they reached the grove of trees, the fog, now rimmed with light, bounced twice at the foot of the trunk of an old oak, almost hidden by bushes and shrubs. As the girls got closer, the phantom rose and settled in the branches. With a silvery arm, it pointed at a hollow in the tree.

"He wants me to climb up there," Kathy said.

Lisa glanced back over her shoulder. "Here they come. Kathy, I'm scared. Mason looks mad."

Kathy pulled herself up into the tree just as Mason lumbered up with Digger close on his heels.

"Run!" Kathy called down to Lisa.

Lisa nodded and took off.

"Hey! Where're you going?" Digger said, out of breath.

Lisa never turned around. She ran along a path of trampled ground that led to the golf course.

Digger looked up at Kathy. "Why are you up there?"

Kathy was so scared that for an instant she couldn't move. She clung to a limb with shaking hands. If she looked down at Mason's face, she would faint. Above her, floating in the upper branches, was the fog. With a surge of courage, Kathy kept climbing upward.

Mason planted a foot against the tree trunk. He grunted and heaved, but he couldn't get up. "Here, lad," he said, grabbing Digger. "Go up and get her."

"Why?"

"No time for questions," Mason snapped.

Digger wrenched himself free and stepped back. "I don't want to."

"She knows where the treasure's buried," Mason said gruffly, staring up at Kathy. "Make her tell us." His dark eyes shot back to Digger and his lips curled into a smile. "Then we can build that ship."

Digger's glasses started to slide down his nose. He jammed them back on with the palm of his hand, then peered up at Kathy. "Do you, Kathy? Know where the treasure is?"

Kathy steeled herself. "Don't come up here, Digger," she pleaded. "Mason's a crook."

Mason reached out to seize Digger under the arms. Digger ducked and slipped through his legs.

Mason whirled around, grabbed the end of a sturdy branch and shook the tree. The tall tree groaned. The glowing phantom slipped past Kathy and dropped to the ground next to Mason.

"You better watch out," Kathy said in a shaky voice.

Mason ignored her and stormed around the tree trunk, trampling down the bushes.

Digger looked to Kathy for direction.

"Go. Now!" Kathy screamed. "Run!"

Mason, muttering to himself, searched on the other side of the tree. Digger removed his glasses and took off at a trot.

"Digger," Mason yelled. "Here's the cross and arrow." He shook a paper in his hand.

Kathy looked down through the branches. Mason had her picture!

"We've found it, lad." He shoved the tip of a shovel into the ground. "Come help me."

But Digger was gone. Mason dug furiously in the hard ground. Kathy, summoning up all the courage she could, started down. The phantom was next to her, growing brighter as Kathy lowered herself. When she had almost reached the bottom, her foot slipped into a hollow. She stopped. Was it safe? If she stayed where she was and Mason came around the other side, he could grab her feet. But he was on the far side and too busy to look up.

Kathy risked it. The other foot made it to the leaf-filled hollow. She felt her right foot resting on something. She shoved it aside with the toe of her shoe. It looked like an old piece of leather crusted with dirt and dried leaves. She picked it up and rubbed it off against her shorts. It was probably a map for the treasure. No time to open it now. She stuffed it inside her waistband. Staying out of Mason's view, she slid down the tree trunk until her feet landed silently on the ground. She crouched there a moment before she darted off, heading for her bike.

CHAPTER
21

At the edge of the field, Kathy stopped abruptly and whirled around. She heard footsteps behind her. Mason was on her trail. She stumbled, then broke into a run. Her skin crawled and her stomach twisted. But Mason couldn't keep up with her. She turned around just in time to see him throw his hands up in disgust. He turned back to the tree and the treasure.

Her bike was where she'd left it. She felt exhausted as she pedaled her way back to the mission. She patted her waistband. The thin leather pouch she'd found in the hollow pressed against her skin. Father Eliot would help her. The treasure belonged to him.

When Kathy wheeled into the mission, Loretta's station wagon was parked in front. Kathy threw her bike down and ran in through the gate. Gram and Loretta stood next to the sanctuary talking to Father Eliot. They all turned at once and Kathy rushed into Gram's waiting arms.

Through tears and sighs, Kathy poured out the story about Mason. "We've got to find Lisa and Digger," she cried.

Father Eliot rushed to his office to make a call. Gram, Loretta, and Kathy piled into the car and Loretta took off in a spray of gravel and dust. At the intersection next to the shopping center, they found Digger. At the Dead End sign, Lisa was just getting on her bike. "I found a man playing golf," she stammered. "He tried to call the restaurant—then the cottage."

Loretta wrapped Lisa in her arms as Father Eliot's car pulled up. Loretta pushed Lisa into her car and went over to the priest's car. She pointed toward the grove.

"Those men with Father Eliot are from the church," she said to Bev a few minutes later, as the men started out through the field. She switched on the ignition. "They suggested we all go home and wait for them there."

On the way to the cottage, everyone spoke at once except Digger. He sat silently in the front seat, squished in between Loretta and Gram. Kathy knew he was sad. Mason had let him down.

"We'll pass on rehearsal today," Loretta said when she let Gram and Kathy out. "I'll take care of the phone calls, Bev. You and Kathy need time to talk."

When Loretta drove off, Gram led Kathy through the house and out onto the deck. Gram sat on a canvas chair and Kathy leaned against the rail. The sun still shone, even though patches of fog hung near the shore.

"Mason needs to be questioned about his inappropriate behavior," Gram said. "How dare he frighten you kids like that."

Kathy nodded slowly. "He's a crook."

"We don't know that for sure," Gram said gently. "Loretta is still waiting to find out what he was up to in that grove. She would like to speak to him personally. Why don't you start by telling me everything you know."

Kathy, more than ready, blurted out the story from beginning to end, starting with the first night of the seance. She told Gram about the phantom, Ambrose, the music box, and the feathers. She ended by explaining how many times she had tried to tell Gram what was happening, but somehow the time was never right.

"I know," Gram said. "It's been difficult for you.

I've been terribly busy with the pageant. And Loretta's problem with La Costa," she added.

"It's not your fault," Kathy said quickly. "When I see things no one else can, most people don't believe me, anyway." She looked down at her feet. "But I did try." She stepped down into the garden. "I'm glad you were at the mission, though. Why were you and Loretta there?"

"Loretta called me from rehearsal when she couldn't find you and Lisa. We looked everywhere. The mission was our last stop."

Kathy came back to the deck with a red rose and gave it to Gram.

"For me? You're the one who should be receiving gifts." She sniffed the flower.

Kathy watched her grandma closely. "Do you believe that the fog is Ambrose? Do you believe in ghosts?"

"Yes, I do. I believe there are ghosts who hold you back, and others who point the way. Obviously, you've been acquainted with a phantom who pointed the way to some unfinished business."

"Gram?"

"Yes, dear?"

"Do you think Mason knew that I could see Ambrose?"

"Anything is possible," Gram said. "With his devotion to early Monterey history, he had to know about Ambrose. If he suspected that you had the gift of sight, and his intent all along has been to find that treasure—" Gram sniffed indignantly. "He probably figured you would lead him to it."

Kathy gave a sigh of relief. Gram believed that Kathy could see things that others didn't. And Gram made her feel that it was okay.

Kathy was silent for a while. Then she said softly, "I'm sorry."

"What for?"

"For not being able to tap dance, being your only granddaughter and all."

Gram reached out. "Come here, Kathy. Don't ever feel that you're a disappointment to me." Kathy crossed the deck and sat down next to her.

Gram put her arm around Kathy's shoulder and gave her a kiss on the forehead. "You are the prettiest, most talented young woman in the world, and don't you ever forget it. Your artwork is wonderful. And you are gifted." She brushed the hair back from Kathy's face. "Some of the Wicklow women have had the power to see with more than just their eyes. And you, my dear, are one of them. I am so proud to be your grandmother."

Kathy laid her head on Gram's shoulder. "You are?" she said happily. "I'll be twelve next year. Do you think I'm getting too old to learn how to tap?"

Gram shook her head. "Never too old," she said

with a happy laugh. "Just ask Loretta. But remember, learn to dance only if you want to. You don't have to learn for anyone else."

She gave Kathy a squeeze. "What's this?" she asked, patting her waist.

Kathy felt the soft leather folder. "I forgot," she said. "I think it's a map for the treasure. I found it in the hollow of the tree." She handed it to Gram.

The doorbell rang. "That's probably Father Eliot and the people from the church," Gram said. "Are you ready to talk to them?"

Kathy stood and straightened her shoulders. "I'll tell them everything I know." On her way to the door, she muttered to herself, "Well, almost everything."

When Kathy returned with Father Eliot and the others, Gram was on her feet. "I've got to call Loretta," she said excitedly. "This is no map. It's the Spanish deed to La Costa!"

CHAPTER

22

Loretta and Lisa arrived at the cottage minutes after Gram called them with the good news. Soon everyone congregated out on the deck.

Father Eliot waited until all the excitement died down before he explained that Mason had vanished by the time they reached the grove of trees. All they found was a roughly dug hole about two feet deep. At the bottom of the hole, they found a layer of old handmade bricks. Apparently Mason couldn't get past the bricks with his shovel, so he took off. "We've got more volunteers from the church over there now using a jackhammer to find out what's under them."

Kathy looked at Lisa knowingly.

Gram looked concerned. "Where do you suppose Mason is now?"

Loretta sat down next to Bev. "Gone," she said angrily. "I hope for good! That old oak with the cross and the arrow stands on the property that belonged to my dead husband's family. The old tree must have been one of the boundaries."

She looked up at Father Eliot. "When your men finish digging, I don't know what they'll find, but I never thought to look there for our deed. That land was taken away from our ancestors by squatters, many, many years ago."

Kathy looked over at Loretta. "Where's Digger?"

Loretta sighed. "He's at the restaurant waiting for Mason to return—sitting there alone. By the time we got home and went upstairs, the door to Mason's room was wide open and most of his belongings were gone. How he ever got back to La Costa before we did, I'll never know." She took a handkerchief from her purse and touched it to her eyes. "Poor Dennis. I still can't believe Mason could do this. Dennis looked up to him. Who would ever have guessed that he was so greedy?"

Kathy spoke up. "Is Mason's ship, the one in the bottle, gone?"

Loretta stopped a moment to think. "Why, I believe it is. Why? Is that important?"

"It is to Digger," Kathy said softly.

After the police finished their report, Loretta and Lisa went home. Loretta vowed to cheer Dennis up if it took all night.

The next evening, Friday, an hour before the pageant, Kathy brushed the last stroke of paint to her pirate scene just as the performers began to arrive at the theater.

When Kathy finally put her brush down and stepped back, Gram stood right there beside her.

"Your scene is wonderful," Gram said. "So realistic." She lifted an eyebrow. "That fella with the knife and the red kerchief sure does look like Mason."

Kathy nodded.

"And that missing little finger?" Gram pointed to the rope. "You must have added that special 'Kathy' touch to it."

Kathy didn't reply.

"Didn't you?" Gram persisted.

Kathy shook her head, then nodded. "I did— and I didn't. First I brushed it out on purpose to make Mason mad. But then that picture in the library book had a pirate with a finger just like his." She looked thoughtful. "I really can't explain it."

Gram patted Kathy's shoulder. "Not everything in this world can be explained. You drew the hand the way you felt it should be, and that's that."

Gram held her arms out from her sides. "Notice anything different?"

"No cane!" Kathy said. "That's great."

Gram smiled. "It's backstage—along with my hanky. I was hoping to be able to walk tonight without any help. And to be rid of that stuffed-up nose. Looks like I made it."

Father Eliot hurriedly climbed the stairs to the stage and joined them. "Have you heard the news?" he asked, catching his breath.

"What?" Gram and Kathy asked together.

"We found the lost church treasure. Buried where Ambrose had placed it, under the old oak. Under the bricks there were golden altar ornaments, jeweled chalices, and ornate candelabras."

Kathy grinned and nodded. "Did they find any feathers?"

The priest looked surprised. "Now, how did you know that? Not only are there feathers, but their quills are filled with gold."

As it got closer to showtime, it looked like everyone who lived on the Monterey Peninsula had come to see the pageant. Kathy went down to the front row and sat next to Digger, who wasn't wearing his glasses.

"Hi, Digger," she said. "How come your face is red on this side?"

He shook his head and turned away.

"No glasses—so you're not talking tonight, huh?" She decided not to push him. Instead she stared up at her scenery panel with a critical eye. Then she studied the other panels depicting Franciscan monks, armed Spanish soldiers, and twisted cypress trees. Wait! There was Lisa's face peeking out between two of the panels. Her face looked blotchy.

The stage lights brightened. The red-haired announcer stepped up to the microphone. "Before the pageant begins, we have a special announcement. A historical treasure from the Carmel Mission has been found. One that has been missing more than a hundred and fifty years, since the pirate Bouchard plundered our bay." She motioned to the front row and the spotlight landed on Kathy and Digger.

"These two young people are responsible for finding it," she said. "Plus one of our performers, Lisa Hererra." She gestured to the side stage entrance and waited. The spotlight moved from the front row to the stage and rested at the entrance until Lisa stepped out.

Everyone clapped heartily as Kathy and Digger climbed the steps to join Lisa.

Suddenly the mayor of Carmel and Father Eliot stood next to them. The applause rose, and the audience gave a standing ovation. Next, Father Eliot stepped forward with three ribbons to be presented in appreciation of their courage.

Kathy, standing in the middle, squeezed Lisa's fingers. Lisa winced. Kathy looked down at Lisa's swollen hand, then over at Digger's. His fingers were just as swollen.

"Poison oak?" she asked.

"Poison oak," Lisa said, glaring at Digger.

The pageant was a giant success. When the three-hour performance was over, the crowd left the Forest Theater humming tunes from the show and cheerfully chatting. Everyone agreed that the painted scenery was beautiful.

"It was fun," Lisa said to Kathy the next morning as they climbed the restaurant stairs to the rotunda. "And I'm glad that Grandma danced."

As they neared Mason's open door, Lisa put her arm out in front of Kathy. "Digger's been up here all night," she whispered. "He's depressed. Guess he misses Mason." They both leaned forward and peeked into the room.

Digger sat slouched in one of the leather chairs next to the empty glass case that had held Mason's guns. "I'm still mad at him for this," she said, pointing to her face, smeared with white lotion. "But we're kind of worried about him, so I'll try to be nice."

Kathy nodded sympathetically. They entered the room together. "Hi Digger," they said in unison.

Digger, his face covered with the same white lotion, stared blankly at the opposite wall. The wall, Kathy noticed, that had once held the talking parrot pendulum clock and the framed receipt.

Lisa went to the big wooden desk and shuffled through the papers. "Looks like he left all of his junky stuff here—and his books," she said, pointing to the bookcase.

"And his spyglass and his telescope," Kathy added, surprised. She turned to face Digger. "Look," she said brightly. "He left them for you."

"I don't want them," Digger finally said in a broken voice, his first words since the ordeal at the old oak tree.

"Maybe not now," Kathy said. "But when you get back to New Mexico..."

He frowned and Kathy thought she saw tears form in his eyes. "Not then either. I just want things to be the way they used to be. Me and Mason building a model ship."

Lisa laughed sarcastically.

Kathy gave Lisa a stern look. "Now that you know how, Digger, you can build your own ship someday. And it will be bigger and better."

Digger stopped staring at the wall and looked at Kathy with a glimmer of hope.

Kathy picked up the brass spyglass, squinted one eye, and pointed the lens at Digger's face.

"This is really powerful," she said. "I can see a little freckle on your ear." She spun around to face the big front window and pointed the spyglass toward the bay. She looked first to the right, then to the left. Moving closer to the window, she let out a gasp. "Lisa," she cried. "Look through the telescope."

"What for?" Lisa asked.

"Quick! Just do it."

By then, Digger had joined them. "Let me see," he demanded.

"Hold on," Lisa said, brushing his hand away from her arm.

"Do you see it?" Kathy asked. She took the glass away from her eye for a moment and stared at Digger. He reached for the spyglass and Kathy gave it to him.

Lisa looked, then stepped back from the telescope. "A sailing schooner," she said. "People sail them here all the time."

"It's not coming this way," Digger said wistfully. "It's probably Mason. Headed westward—off to the Komodo Island."

"Right," Lisa said. "And when he gets there he'll send you a dragon."

Kathy turned to Digger. "That could happen,"

she said. "Then you could put it next to your dinosaur egg in New Mexico."

Loretta called up from downstairs. "*Niños.* Lunch is ready. Come and eat."

Digger set the spyglass down on the desk and filed out after Lisa. Lisa stopped and poked her head through the door. "Come on, Kathy. Let's eat."

"In a minute," Kathy said. "Save me a taco."

When they had gone, Kathy moved closer to the front window. Incredible! Even without the spyglass, she could see the ship and the name painted in black on the hull, as clearly as if she were standing beneath the pageant scenery.

La Frigata Negra. The black ship.

Seeing the ship out there, its sails billowing in the sunlight, she felt goose bumps on her arms. She carefully removed a feather from her shorts pocket. As she twirled the quill slowly, the music box tune echoed softly through the room.

She turned and her eyes scanned the walls. Nothing. Turning back to the window, she pushed the feather behind her ear and pressed her forehead against the glass. She stared out at the bay. On the horizon, a wall of fog connected the sea and the sky.

Should she tell Digger that she knew the name of the ship? And how about Lisa? They had helped each other when they were too scared to stand alone. She watched until the ship disappeared into the fog. At first, when Kathy had arrived at Gram's cottage, she had hated the fog. Now she felt protected by it. She turned away from the window. Maybe she didn't have to decide today who and what she would tell. Hadn't Gram said that not everything in this world could be explained? She gave the room one more quick look and headed for the door.

THE END